TELLING TALES

short stories
by
SARA MAITLAND

THE JOURNEYMAN PRESS
LONDON & WEST NYACK

First published 1983 by the Journeyman Press Limited,
97 Ferme Park Road, Crouch End, London, N8 9SA, and
17 Old Mill Road, West Nyack, NY 10994, USA

1 2 3 4 5 6 7 8 9 10

Copyright © by Sara Maitland, 1983

0 904526 87 9 *cased*
0 904526 86 0 *paper*

Acknowledgements

My thanks are due to the following publishers: *Time Out* for
'The Loveliness of the Long Distance Runner'; Faber and
Faber, *Introduction 5*, for 'Hyppolita' and 'An Edwardian
Tableau'; *Bananas* for 'Blessed are those who mourn',
'Conquistador' and 'Andromeda'; *Hecate* (Australia) for
'Lilith' and 'The Dreams of the Papess Joan'.

I would also like to thank Robin Furneaux for *The Amazon:
The Story of a Great River* which provided the factual
material for 'Conquistador', and to Michelene Wandor who
gave me a lot of help with the manuscript.

Cover design by Caroline Grimshaw

Printed in Great Britain by
Biddles Ltd, Guildford, Surrey

Telling Tales

4, Beaufort Road,
Broomhill,
Sheffield, S10 2ST
Tel: 0742 666539

Contents

For Desiree Martin, with love

Of Deborah and Jael

AFTERWARDS DEBORAH THE Prophetess, the Judge in Israel, made a song for Jael the Kenite. Using her public authority, she sang of Jael, blessed above all women, extolling her above all people. She made the song because they were friends, and because they had both come a long way to find that friendship, they who had never had a friend before. They had stood side by side, their arms raised in victory, and they had not been afraid. That love and joy and strength were in the song.

It was a rich strong song and its rhythms were the ancient sturdy ones of women's work, of spinning and weaving and pounding and stirring. Although it was a song of a great victory the men never came to love and use it, but the women sang it often as they worked and so remembered. When their men asked for water and were tenderly given milk, when they poured the yellow goat curds into bowls, when they had occasion to move camp and so pull up the wooden tent-pegs, or to clean and refurbish their menfolks' hammers, they would pause, then sing a phrase or two from the song that Deborah made for Jael, and smile and so remember.

Jael fondles the tent-peg, one hand wrapped firmly around it, the other stroking the pointed end carressingly. She feels the weight of the hammer in her hand, resistant, solid, heavy, beautiful. Jael looks at Sisera asleep, his noble head turned slightly sideways on the pillow she has laid out for him, his hair smoothed back from his forehead — by her, by her. Between the thick dark oiled tresses of his head and the silky scented growth of his beard, his temple glows sweetly in the moonlight. He is a man, he is a king, bred and raised on royal food. He is the most powerful, the most beautiful man she has ever seen. He is more beautiful than she could imagine, than her husband could conceive of being, more manly, more virile; even asleep he carries his authority, the dreams he dreams are regal. He came to her tent without doubts, confident in his own powerfulness. He had asked for water and she had given him milk, she had brought him curds in a lordly bowl. And who would do otherwise or less for such a man. For the first time in her life it is a joy to service man, because this is a man who has earned service by his very existing. Before she places the point of the peg against that soft glowing skin she kisses the spot with tenderness, a melting joy, that she had not known she could feel. She goes out of the tent and looks at the roughness of the mountains, the shagged piles of additional darkness against the dark sky; she hears the warmth that seeps out from the goats at night, she smells the heavy round moon sigh towards its setting, she sees the burning stars wheeling against the desert sky. Her skin seems newly alive in the coolness. It is very silent. She is very joyful.

Back in the tent she does not hesitate: the weight of the hammer is with her now, the pointed stick no longer alien but a part of her person. With her very first hammer blow she breaks clean through the white skin, penetrates deep into the bone, the point is finding its own pathway into the depths of the man. He groans once, unable to resist the strength behind her stroke and she has heard that groan before. She breaks through her own carefulness, becomes beserk, and long after it is necessary, bang, bang, bang, rhythmical and powerful. She bangs, in and in. The blood and the flesh flow out over the sheep-skin coverlet, over the pillow, she is delighted by her own power. Bang, bang, bang, bang. Deeper and stronger. Her moment in history, her song, her story, her revenge.

After, she sinks exhausted against the bedding, lying close to the bleeding corpse, to what had once been a king, a beautiful and powerful man, before he met her. She sees that with his last reflex he has shat himself, and worn out by her own excitement, she giggles: not very regal, not very manly, and she — the middle-aged wife of Heber, a simple tent woman and goatherd — she has done this to the greatest king in all the world. Looking at the mess, the best sheets and skins unusable ever again, the elaborate embroidered clothes he wore, the oiled gold-braided hair all ruined with blood and fragments of bone, looking at the mess she has her most intense moment of triumph. When her husband returns from his war and sees what she has done he will be very very frightened, of her, of her.

Deborah the Prophetess had looked at the slaughter on the field beneath Mount Tabor and had laughed. She had looked so at her husband many times but had never before felt the freedom to laugh aloud. But this was all her own doing: the broken chariots, the great army of Sisera put to the sword, and the slow mounting chants of victory from the tribes. All her own doing: with the authority that she had earned and that they had given her she had summoned Barak to her at her judgement seat under the palm between Ramah and Bethel. She had made him into a general, by prophesy, jeers and good advice, and had called together an army for him. She had gone with that army, one of them and their leader, she had been Barak's courage and the courage of the whole armed force of the tribes of Israel. It had been something to be proud of and she had been proud and she had laughed. But now she stands at the tent of Jael and her laughter is drowned in a fiercer joy. Suddenly, for the first time in all her life, it does not matter to her that she is an ugly woman; she had wept about it through her youth, and grieved it silently through her adult life and now it does not matter any more. Her words are strong and beautiful instead: she has delivered the mighty Sisera into the hands of a woman.

Barak, general of the victorious army of the Israelites, conqueror of the greatest king the world has ever known, adulated by his troops and his countrymen, battle-honoured, young, handsome and admired, is very frightened. Things have got out of his control and he does not like it. It is the doing of that old witch Deborah, who has stolen from him his triumph and left him shaken with fear. The battle itself had never scared him, not in the least, the Lord of Armies had fought for him, he was the defender of the noble truth, the mysterious name of Yahweh, he was the hand of the Power that drowned the Egyptians, the inheritor of the Sword of the Lord. On the battle field he had known his own manhood, the rush of the charge from Mount Tabor, he had tasted the admiration of his enemies, the strong wind of carnage that encourages a man, that builds him up and reminds him of his birthright. But now he has to look at the tent standing so mild by its stream, the goats and sheep softly, sweetly picking at the sparse mountain grass, and he feels sick with his fear. He does not want to have to go back into that tent, to look at that crazy little woman and the bloody mess, the disgusting remains of another great man and worthy enemy.

Deborah and Jael look at each other, they smile at each other — they are friends. They look at the smashed head of Sisera, the blood soaked bedding, the tent-peg still standing upright in the remains, and they grin. They reach out hands, unspeaking, almost shy with excitement, and touch each other very gently. They know their husbands will never want to touch them again. They know who the enemy is. They grin again, and then laugh, breathing in the exhilarating stink of fear that comes to their nostrils. When they walk together out of the tent, bending gracefully together to avoid the door hanging, they rejoice because the whole army, the whole victorious, manic, excited exultant army is silent with fear.

Deborah the Prophetess takes the arm of Jael, just above the wrist and holds up her right hand for all the men in the army to see. She had told them that God would deliver Sisera into the hand of a woman, that the stars in their courses would fight against Sisera. She had spoken with authority, and they have to know it. Jael is smaller, lighter than Deborah, who can hold up her friend's clenched fist without strain, and show the men the victor, the despoiler, the claimer of the spoils. Deborah laughs, Jael laughs, but the men watch in silence. What is the source of the joy that lights up these women? What are the words of the song they will sing together? What power drove the hand that drove the nail? The men cannot avoid seeing the women, they cannot help feeling the hatred and the joy. They are sick with fear.

The Loveliness of the Long Distance Runner

I SIT AT my desk and make a list of all the things I am not going to think about for the next four and a half hours. Although it is still early the day is conducive to laziness — hot and golden. I am determined that I will not be lazy. The list reads:

1. My lover is running in an organised marathon race. I hate it.
2. Pheidippides, the Greek who ran the first Marathon, dropped dead at the end of it. And his marathon was four miles shorter than hers is going to be. There is also heat stroke, torn achilles tendons, shin splints and cramp. Any and all of which, including the first option, will serve her right. And will also break my heart.
3. The women who are going to support her, love her, pour water down her back and drinks down her throat are not me. I am jealous of them.
4. Marathon running is a goddam competitive, sexist, lousy thing to do.
5. My lover has the most beautiful body in the world. Because she runs. I fell in love with her because she had the most beautiful body I had ever seen. What, when it comes down to it, is the difference between my devouring of her as a sex-object and her competitive running? Anyway she says that she does not run competitively. Anyway I say that I do not any longer love her just because she has the most beautiful body.

Now she will be doing her warm-up exercises. I know these well, as she does them every day. She was doing them the first time I saw her. I had gone to the country to stay the weekend with her sister, who's a lawyer colleague of mine and a good friend. We were doing some work together. We were sitting in her living room and she was feeding her baby and Jane came in, in running shorts, T-shirt and yards and yards of leg. Katy had often joked about her sister who was a games mistress in an all-girls' school, and I assumed that this was she. Standing by the front door, with the sun on her hair, she started these amazing exercises. She

stretched herself from the waist and put her hands flat on the
floor; she took her slender foot in her hand and bent over backwards. The blue shorts strained slightly; there was nothing spare
on her, just miles and miles of tight, hard, thin muscle. And as she
exhibited all this peerless flesh she chatted casually of this and
that — how's the baby, and where she was going to run. She
disappeared through the door. I said to Katy,
'Does she know I'm gay?'
Katy grinned and said, 'Oh, yes.'
'I feel set-up.'
'That's what they're called — setting-up exercises.'
I felt very angry. Katy laughed and said, 'She is too.'
'Is what?' I asked.
'Gay.' I melted into a pool of desire.

*It's better to have started. The pre-race excitement makes me feel
a little sick. Tension. But also . . . people punching the air and
shouting 'Let's go, let's go.' Psyching themselves up. Casing each
other out. Who's better than who? Don't like it. Don't want to do
it. Wish I hadn't worn this T-shirt. It has 'I am a feminist jogger'
on it. Beth and Emma gave it to me. Turns people on though.
Men. Not on to me but on to beating me. I won't care. There's a
high on starting though, crossing the line. Good to be going,
good to have got here. Doesn't feel different because someone
has called it a marathon, rather than a good long run. Keep it
that way. But I would like to break three and a half hours. Step
by step. Feel good. Fitter than I've ever been in my life, and I like
it. Don't care what Sally says. Mad to despise body when she
loves it so. Dualist. I like running. Like me running. Space and
good feeling. Want to run clear of this crowd — too many
people, too many paces. Want to find someone to run my own
pace with. Have to wait. Pace; endurance; deferment of pleasure; patience; power. Sally ought to like it — likes the benefits
alright. Bloke nearby wearing a T-shirt that reads, 'Runners
make the best lovers'. He grins at me. Bastard. I'll show him: run
for the Women's Movement. A trick. Keep the rules. My number
one rule is 'run for yourself.' But I bet I can run faster than him.*

*Hurt myself running once, because of that. Ran a ten-mile
race, years ago, with Annie, meant to be a fun-run and no
sweat. There was this jock; a real pig; he kept passing us, daw-
dling, letting us pass him, passing again. And every time these
remarks — the vaseline stains from our nipples, or women*

getting him too turned on to run. Stuff like that; and finally he runs off, all sprightly and tough, patronising. We ran on. Came into the last mile or so and there he was in front of us, tiring. I could see he was tired. 'Shall we?' I said to Annie, but she was tired too. 'Go on then,' she was laughing at me, and I did. Hitched up a gear or two, felt great, zoomed down the hill after him, cruised alongside, made it look easy, said, 'Hello, sweet-heart, you look tired' and sailed on. Grinned back over my shoulder, he had to know who it was, and pulled a muscle in my neck. Didn't care — he was really pissed off. Glided over the finishing line and felt great for twenty minutes. Then I felt bad; should have known better — my neck hurt like hell, my legs cramped from over-running. But it wasn't just physical. Felt bad mentally. Playing those games.

Not today. Just run and feel good. Run into your own body and feel it. Feel road meeting foot, one by one, a good feeling. Wish Sally knew why I do it. Pray she'll come and see me finish. She won't. Stubborn bitch. Won't think about that. Just check leg muscles and pace and watch your ankles. Run.

If she likes to run that much of course I don't mind. It's nice some evenings when she goes out, and comes back and lies in the bath. A good salty woman. A flavour that I like. But I can't accept this marathon business: who wants to run 26 miles and 385 yards, in a competitive race? Jane does. For the last three months at least our lives have been taken over by those 26 miles, what we eat, what we do, where we go, and I have learned to hate every one of them. I've tried, 'Why?' I've asked over and over again; but she just says things like, 'because it's there, the ultimate.' Or 'Just once Sally, I'll never do it again.' I *bet* I think viciously. Sometimes she rational-ises: women have to do it. Or, it's important to the women she teaches. Or, it has to be a race because nowhere else is set up for it: you need the other runners, the solidarity, the motivation. 'Call it sisterhood. You can't do it alone. You need . . .' And I interrupt and say, 'You need the competition; you need people to beat. Can't you see?' And she says, 'You're wrong. You're also talking about something you know nothing about. So shut up. You'll just have to believe me: you need the other runners and mostly they need you and want you to finish. And the crowd wants you to finish, they say. I want to experience that solidarity, of other people wanting you to do what you want to do.' Which is a slap in the face for me, because I don't want her to do what she wants to do.

And yet — I love the leanness of her, which is a gift to me from marathon training. I love what her body is and what it can do, and go on doing and not be tired by doing. She has the most beautiful legs, hard, stripped down, with no wastage and her Achilles' tendons are like flexible rock. Running does that for her. And then I think, damn, damn, damn. I will not love her for those reasons; but I will love her because she is tough and enduring and wryly ironic. Because she is clear about what she wants and prepared to go through great pain to get it; and because her mind is clear, careful and still open to complexity. She wants to stop being a Phys. Ed. teacher because now that women are getting as much money for athletic programmes the authorities suddenly demand that they should get into competition, winning trips. Whereas when she started it was fun for her and for women being together as women, doing the things they had been laughed at for, as children.

She says I'm a dualist and she laughs at me. She says I want to separate body and soul while she runs them together. When she runs she thinks: not ABC like I think with my tidy well-trained mind, but in flashes — she'll trot out with some problem and run 12 or 15 miles and come home with the kinks smoothed out. She says that after eight or ten miles she hits a euphoric high — grows free — like meditation or something, but better. She tells me that I get steamed up through a combination of tension and inactivity. She can run out that stress and be perfectly relaxed while perfectly active. She comes clean. Ten or twelve miles at about eight minutes per mile: about where she'll be getting to now.

I have spent another half hour thinking about the things I was not going to think about. Tension and inactivity. I cannot concentrate the mind.

When I bend my head forward and Emma squeezes the sponge onto my neck, I can feel each separate drop of water flow down my back or over my shoulders and down between my breasts. I listen to my heart beat and it seems strong and sturdy. As I turn Emma's wrist to see her watch her blue veins seem translucent and fine. Mine seem like strong wires conducting energy. I don't want to drink and have it lying there in my stomach, but I know I should. Obedient, giving over to Emma, I suck the bottle. Tell myself I owe it to her. Her parents did not want her to spend a hot Saturday afternoon nursing her games' teacher. When I'm back in rhythm I feel the benefits of the drink. Emma is a good kid. Her parents' un-named suspicions are correct. I was in love with a games' teacher once. She was a big strong woman, full of energy. I pretended to share what the others thought and mocked her. We called her Tarzan and how I loved her. In secret dreams I wanted to be with her. 'You Tarzan, me Jane,' I would mutter, contemplating her badly-shaved underarms, and would fly with her through green trees, swing on lianas of delight. She was my first love; she helped make me a strong woman. The beauty, the immensity of her. When we swam she would hover over the side of the pool and as I looked up through the broken, sparkly water there she would be hauling me through with her strength.

Like Sally hauls me through bad dreams, looming over me in the night as I breathe up through the broken darkness. She hauls me through muddle with her sparkly mind. Her mind floats, green with sequinned points of fire. Sally's mind. Lovely. My mind wears Nike running shoes with the neat white flash curling back on itself. It fits well and leaves room for my toes to flex. If I weren't a games' teacher I could be a feminist chiropodist — or a midwife. Teach other women the contours of their own bodies — show them the new places where their bodies can take them. Sally doesn't want to be taken — only in the head. Sex of course is hardly in her head. In the heart? My heart beats nearly 20 pulses a minute slower than hers: we test them together lying in the darkness, together. 'You'll die, you shit,' I want to yell at her. 'You'll die and leave me. Your heart isn't strong enough.' I never say it. Nice if your hearts matched. The Zulu warrior women could run fifty miles a day and fight at the end of it. Fifty miles together, perfectly in step, so the veldt drummed with it. Did their hearts beat as one? My heart can beat with theirs, slow and strong and efficient — pumping energy.

Jane de Chantal, after whom I was named, must have been a jogger. She first saw the Sacred Heart — how else could she have known that slow, rich stroke which is at the heart of everything? Especially back then when the idea of heart meant only emotions. But she was right. The body, the heart at the heart of it all: no brain, no clitoris without that strong slow heart. Thesis: was a seventeenth century nun the first jogger? Come on; this is rubbish. Think about footstrike and stride length. Not this garbage. Only one Swedish garbage-collector, in the whole history of Swedish municipal rubbish collection, has ever worked through to retirement age — what perseverance, endurance. What a man. Person. Say garbage person. Sally says so. Love her. Damn her. She is my princess. I'm the younger son (say person) in the fairy story. But running is my wise animal. If I'm nice to my running it will give me good advice on how to win the princess. Float with it. Love it. Love her. There has to be a clue.

Emma is here again. Car? Bicycle? She can't have run it. She and Beth come out and give me another drink, wipe my face. Lovely hands. I come down and look around. After twenty miles they say there are two sorts of smiles among runners — the smiles of those who are suffering and the smiles of those who aren't. 'You're running too fast,' says Beth, 'You're too high. Pace yourself, you silly twit. You're going to hurt.' 'No,' I say, 'I'm feeling good.' But I know she's right. Discipline counts. Self-discipline, but Beth will help with that. 'We need you to finish,' says Emma. 'Of course she'll finish,' says Beth. I love them and I run away from them, my mouth feeling good with orange juice and soda water. Ought to have been Sally though. Source of sweetness. How could she do this to me? How could she leave me? Desert me in the desert. Make a desert. This is my quest — my princess should be here. Princess: she'd hate that. I hate that. Running is disgusting; makes you think those thoughts. I hurt. I hurt and I am tired. They have lots of advice for this point in a marathon. They say think of all the months that are wasted if you stop now. But not wasted because I enjoyed them. They say, whoever wanted it to be easy? I did. They say, think of that man who runs marathons with only one leg. And that's meant to be inspirational. He's mad. We're all mad. There's no reason but pride. Well, pride then. Pride and the thought of Sally suppressing her gloating if I go home and say it hurt too much. I need a good reason to run into and through this tiredness.

Something stabs my eyes with orange. Nothing really hurt before but now it hurts. Takes me all of three paces to locate the hurt: cramp in the upper thighs. Sally's fault; I think of her and tense up. Ridiculous. But I'll be damned if I quit now. Run into the pain; I know it will go away and I don't believe it. Keep breathing steadily. It hurts. I know it hurts, shut up, shut up, shut up. Who cares if it hurts? I do. Don't do this. Seek out a shirt in front of you and look at the number. Keep looking at the number. 297. Do some sums with that. Can't think of any. Not divisible by 2, or 3, or 5. Nor 7. 9. 9 into 29 goes 3. 3 and carry 2. 9 into 27. Always works. If you can divide by something the cramp goes away. Is that where women go in childbirth — into the place of charms? All gay women should run marathons —

*gives them solidarity with their labouring sisters. I feel sick
instead. I look ahead and there is nothing but the long hill.
Heartbreaking. I cannot.*

*Shirt 297 belongs to a woman, a little older than me perhaps.
I run beside her, she is tired too. I feel better and we run together.
We exchange a smile. Ignore the fact that catching up with her
gives me a lift. We exchange another smile. She is slowing. She
grins and deliberately reduces her pace so that I can go ahead
without feeling bad. That's love. I love her. I want to turn round,
jog back and say, 'I will leave my lover for you.' 'Dear Sally,' I
will write, 'I am leaving you for a lady who' (and Sally's mental
red pencil will correct to 'whom') 'I met during the marathon
and unlike you she was nice and generous to me.' Alternative
letter, 'Dear Sally, I have quit because long distance running
brings you up against difficulties and cramps and I cannot take
the pain.' Perseverance, endurance, patience and accepting love
are part of running a marathon. She won't see it. Damn her.*

*Must be getting near now because there's a crowd watching.
They'll laugh at me. 'Use the crowd,' say those who've been here
before. 'They want you to finish. Use that.' Lies. Sally doesn't
want me to finish. What sort of princess doesn't want the quest
finished? Wants things cool and easy? Well pardon me, your
Royal Highness. Royal Highness: the marathon is 26 miles and
385 yards long because some princess wanted to see the start of
the 1908 Olympic Marathon from Windsor Palace and the
finish from her box in the White City Stadium. Two miles longer
than before. Now standardised. By appointment. Damn the
Royal Princess. Damn Sally.*

Finally I accept that I'm not going to do any work today. It takes
me several more minutes to accept what that means — that I'm
involved in that bloody race. People tend, I notice, to equate
accepting with liking — but it's not that simple. I don't like it. But,
accepting, I get the car out and drive to the shops and buy the
most expensive bath oil I can find. It's so expensive that the box is
perfectly modest — no advertising, no half-naked women. I like
half-naked women as a matter of fact, but there are such things as
principles. Impulsively I also buy some matching lotion, thinking
that I will rub it on her feet tonight. Jane's long slender feet are
one part of her body that owe nothing to running. This fact alone
is enough to turn me into a foot fetishist.

After I have bought the stuff and slavered a bit over the thought of rubbing it into her poor battered feet (I worked it out once. Each foot hits the ground about 800 times per mile. The force of the impact is three times her weight. 122 pounds times 800 times 26 miles. It does not bear thinking about.) I realise the implications of rubbing sweet ointment into the tired feet of the beloved person. At first I am embarassed and then I think, well Mary Magdalen is one way through the sex-object, true love dichotomy. Endurance, perseverance, love. She must have thought the crucifixion a bit mad too. Having got this far in acceptance I think that I might as well go down to the finish and make her happy. We've come a long way together. So I get back into the car and do just that.

It is true, actually. In the last few miles the crowd holds you together. This is not the noble hero against the world. Did I want that? But this is better. A little kid ducked under the rope and gave me a half-eaten ice-lolly — raspberry flavour. Didn't want it. Couldn't refuse such an act of love. Took it. Felt fine. Smiled. She smiled back. It was a joy. Thank you sister. The people roar for you, hold you through the sweat and the tears. They have no faces. The finishing line just is. Is there. You are meant to raise your arms and shout, 'Rejoice, we conquer' as you cross it. Like Pheidippides did when he entered Athens and history. And death. But all I think is 'Christ, I've let my anti-gravity muscles get tight.' They hurt. Sally is here. I don't believe it. Beth drapes a towel over my shoulders without making me stop moving. Emma appears, squeaking, 'Three hours, 26 and a half. That's great. That's bloody great.' I don't care. Sally has cool soft arms. I look for them. They hold me. 'This is a sentimental ending', I try to say. I'm dry. Beth gives me a beer. I cannot pour it properly. It flows over my chin, soft and cold, blissfully cold. I manage a grin and it spreads all over me. I feel great. I lean against Sally again. I say, 'Never, never again.' She grins back and, not without irony, says, 'Rejoice, we conquer.'

True North

FAR NORTH, INSIDE the ice circle, in the land of the long night, lived two women. One was a young woman and one was an old woman. The old woman must have known how they came to be living there, on their own, so far away from other people, but she never said. The young woman did not know — she remembered no other view than the long lifting of the snow banks and the chopped ragged ice in the sea below their home.

Because there was no one else they did not need names for each other and used none. Because they had no community they did not need to name their relationship either, and they did not do so. They never used the words mother or daughter or friend or sister or aunt, niece, cousin, lover. They just lived there together. Because there was no one to see they did not know that the young woman was very beautiful and that the old woman was not. They knew that the old woman was full of ancient knowledge and useful skills, was wise in the ways of weather and seals, and knew all the hundred words for snow. The young woman was strong and tough and could run all day, a slow steady lope across the snow, in pursuit of the moose herds, and she could crawl and slither over the ice after seals and polar bears. And in the evenings the old woman could tell stories about the Seal Queen, and the lemmings maddened by each other and the winter fever who rushed into the sea; and her gums could chew, her hands could carve and her fingers could sew and plait and skin and braid. The young woman could sing and dance and let down her beautiful long hair and comb the thick dark mess until it glowed and sparkled with strange lights. And so they lived happily for a long time.

When spring comes inside the ice circle it is not with long rains and sweet emerging greenness. Instead there is the strange sound of the deep ice crashing and gonging as it it breaks up — howling at night as it shifts and moves at last. The skeins of geese overhead break the stillness of the air with the powerful rush of their homecoming; and the she-seals are fat with promise and contentment. The light begins to seep back into the air; hardly noticed at first, the blubber lamp pales and the distant ice floes take on specific shapes. Where the winter freeze humped and pressured the sea into strange designs there is a new flatness smoothing itself back into water, but slowly.

And one year, with the spring, came something new. One morning when the young woman left the warmth of the ice house she saw, far away across the whiteness a new shape she had never seen before and heard, borne on the motionless air, a new noise, a swish-swish. The shape was dark and tall and it was not silent. In fear she watched a while and the shape came nearer. She turned back into the ice house and told the old woman. And the old woman wrapped a polar fur around herself and came out. The shape had come nearer; it had a strange rising and falling gait, not the smoothness of an animal but rhythmic, lilting like the tune from a song. The shape was coming towards them directly and with purpose and both women were afraid, though for very different reasons: the young woman was afraid because she did not know what the shape was. The old woman was afraid because she did. It was a man.

He was a young man, tall and handsome. He was an ice traveller. He had spent the winter far from his village, all alone, because of a courageous but foolish error of judgement which had taken him too far to get back before the snow storms and the darkness had come. He had wintered far from his own people and was now on his way home. He was surprised to discover this ice house; he had not known that anyone could go away and live so far from the village. Now, swishing on his wide snow shoes, swinging each leg wide of the other, his pack on his back, he came across the snow plateau and, seeing the smoke, thought of singing and company and warm meals cooked by someone not himself and of a few days rest before he went on with his endless ice travelling.

The two women stood at the door of their home. With the necessary courtesy of people who live in such cruel terrain it never occurred to them that they would not welcome him and feed him with whatever they had available and keep him in comfort until he was ready to travel again. In the pale light of the mid-morning he came towards them, slowly, swinging and swishing, and they stood there and waited for him. And when he came up they took him by the arms and led him into their home, and all three of them stood unwinding from their fur clothes in the light of the blubber oil lamp. And as she took off her seal skin jacket and pulled back her fur-rimmed hood the young woman learned at last that she was beautiful, because his eyes told her so. And as she sunk to her haunches to tend the cooking the old woman knew that she was old and ugly, because his eyes did not even turn from the young woman.

Of course the young man loved the young woman; and the young woman loved the young man. Nothing else was possible with the spring crashing into life around them and both of them strangers to the other, and the young woman had never seen a man before and the young man was far from home on a courageous but foolish journey. Yes, they loved each other and the young man took the young woman to wife there in the ice house, on the fullness of the spring tides in front of the old woman and she said not a word, but squatted lower over the cooking pot and faded as the summer came. She could not hate the young woman, because she had known and lived with her for far too long and she could not hate the young man because she could see the rightness of this mating. But her sleep was disturbed by their loving and then by the dreams that came to her afterwards.

In some ways it was good to have the young man with them. With two hunters, both active and tireless and whose bodies know the curves and thoughts of each other's, there is hunting possible which cannot be done alone, and the piles of fur beside the house mounted and the young man talked of trading and possessions that the women knew nothing about — of drink that turned your head to fire and allowed you to meet the ancestors again and fight with the monsters; of fishing hooks and needles so fine and strong that they seemed magical; of colours and ribbons and beads and clothes that the women thought were parts of stories and not real though he told them over and over again. He took the old woman's skins in his hands and admired them and said that she had more skill with the knife than anyone, man or woman, he had ever seen and the skins that she handled would fetch higher prices. And he picked up the carvings she did, in bone and rock, marvelling how the walrus and the bear and the fish were revealed growing there. These too they could trade and he described the things that he and the young woman could have if they sold the carvings the old woman had made. And she who had carved for delight alone, through the long winter, wanted to snatch back her animals from his hands and hide them, but she did not. She did not because the muscles on his neck stood out like the sinews of the moose, and his legs were sturdy, strong and planted firmly in the ground, and his hands were driving into her heart and gut with their strength and beauty, and because the white horn of his nails made her think of the new moon. But she did not trust him.

And she was right. One day the young woman came to her and said that they were going away. She did not think about the old woman left alone in the ice house when winter came again; she did not think about the cold wind and the wildness to be endured alone. She said that he had made a sledge for her, each runner the rib of a great he-walrus that the young man had killed for her; he had worked on the sledge secretly when the old woman thought that he was hunting or walking or fishing. She said the sledge was the most beautiful thing she had ever seen; each runner was intricately carved; the seat was lined with pale fur; the seal sinews were so strong and taut that she would ride without a jolt across the frozen wastes. He would take her to his village and buy for her beads and jewels and garments worthy of her beauty. The young woman told the old woman that her husband was going to take her away from this dreary desolation, and this empty lonely life, and bring her to a place where her beauty would be appreciated and reflect credit on him. She told the old woman also that there was a child growing in her, that she hoped for a son as lithe and fine and strong as the young man, that she would have a son and a place where her beauty could be admired.

She desired the beauty of the young woman; she desired the child of the young woman; she desired the husband of the young woman; and she had little enough to do all day except feed those desires. So that ate into her, like the ice of the approaching autumn, creeping up the rivers of her blood. Soon the couple must be gone, because the courage and foolishness of the young man were diminished by the loveliness of his wife and his tenderness for her, and he wanted to be in his village safe and certain before the hard weather and the long night came. The time was approaching when the old woman could wait no longer. One day the young man was gone from the house, so the old woman said to the young woman that it was a long, long time since she had braided up that beautiful hair. She said that they should prepare a special feast for the young man and that the young woman must look her most beautiful. The young woman was pleased; she felt that the old woman had not entered into her joy and had withdrawn from her recently so she was happy to find that she had been mistaken. So she unpinned her long hair and sat cross-legged on the floor at the feet of the old woman. The old woman took the comb made from bone which she had carved many years ago for the young woman and began to comb her hair. And she combed and combed. She revelled in the last time in that living loveliness; the hair shone and shook in the light of the lamp and sparkled like the sea-deep does in mid summer when it is crazed by the lights of the under world that float up and dance on the surface. The young woman told her to hurry, eager to see her beauty in the admiration of the young man. So then the old woman took the hair and began to twist and braid it into a fat rope, and she took the rope and wound it round the young woman's lovely cream coloured neck and pulled and pulled, tighter and tighter, until the young woman was dead. Then she took her little hand knife, which she had made herself for skinning, down from the wall and, using all of her immense and practised skill, she skinned the young woman's face, not spoiling the hair which was both lovely and necessary, not pulling out one eyelash nor missing the soft curves of lip and cheek. And when the young woman was faceless and bloody she dragged her out of the house and buried her in the soft snow of a drift not far away. Then she took a broom and swept the house and the snow with great attention so that no blood and no drag lines and no mess could be seen. Then she took a soft seal skin shift that she had made herself for the young woman and put it on; its gentle folds caressed her skin and everything seemed possible for her. She washed in ice water, the coldness of it bracing her joyfully. After all that she took the skin from the face of the young woman and with the delicate practice of the years smoothed the young woman's face over her own. Its lovely pliability covered the wrinkles and jutting bones of her old, ugly face; she pulled the creamy skin of the neck down as far as it would go, securing it with an ivory pin to the top of the soft shift; she tugged the heavy mass of hair back over her own thinning greasy locks and shook her head so that it fell loose again covering the seam-lines. And then she lay on the bed that the young couple had made themselves, and covered herself with the furs and skins under which they lay night after night, leaving her outside. The thought of what she had done warmed her; the thought of what was coming heated her. She lay there waiting, ready and eager.

The young man came home. She heard the gentle rhythm of his

snow shoes; she heard him banging off the spare snow and stomping about outside the house; she heard his muffled breath as he pulled his skin-jacket over his head; she heard the soft whistle that he always made when he was tired but pleased with himself. He came in. And seeing her lying on the bed all beautiful and waiting for him, he smiled. Where was the old one he asked. And she told him that she had gone to the beach to look for a special stone for a special carving, to be a present for them at their departure, a very special carving as a bride gift and a gift for the child. The young man said that that was good because such a carving by the old hag would fetch a good price from some white-skinned collector and he laughed. The old woman would be gone for hours on such a task. The young man tugged at his boots; then he pulled off his shift, his trousers. His chest was muscled and beautiful, his loins were leaping for his bride, he fell upon her and she, kicking back the blankets, received him in her eagerness. He plunged into her body and she responded with delight. He was so far into his joy and lust that he did not notice the changed body. He plunged and bucked like the melting of a river when the great chunks of ice are hurled suddenly into the sea; he melted into her like the full tide of spring; and she leaped up for him like a young seal taking to the water for the first time. He rode her like the porpoise schools, she held him like the ocean deep. There was a love and a knowing in them both.

He worked her like an old bull walrus and it was hot hard work and at last he was done and lifted his head and smiled down into her eyes. And the sweat from his joyful labour dripped from his forehead down the fringe of his black hair and fell onto her face. It shrivelled the skin, because the old woman had not had time for proper curing. The skin of the young woman shrank and curled away from the face of the old woman. Where it was secured at the neck with the ivory pin it tore away; from around her mouth the lips peeled back revealing her thin tired gums. The bones of her cheeks broke through the tenderness of the young woman's skin. The tears that sprang in her eyes rolled away the young woman's soft velvet and uncovered the harsh wrinkles. The hair-line parted under the strain — the thick hair falling backwards onto the pile of bed-skins, the forehead dissolving, shrinking, disappearing.

With his hands he completed the work his sweat had begun, scrabbling at her face, scratching her, making her bleed. She herself did not move. Still naked, still lying on her, his lower body still replete with joy, the horror came into his eyes. The young man screamed and leapt to his feet; he grabbed for his shift, his breeches and boots and rushed out into the gathering gloom. She heard him retching and gasping as he fumbled the straps of his snow shoes. She heard his heaves and moans as he gathered what was necessary from around him. At last she heard the swishing, swishing mixed with his horror, repulsion and guilt. The noises died away into the twilight, diminishing, fading and finally, after many many minutes, finally gone.

And then the old woman was alone.

Natural Freaks

The quotations in this text are verbatim from the *Catalogue of Potter's Museum of Curiosity*, which was founded in 1861. The core of the collection is the handiwork of the taxidermist Walter Potter (1835–1918): as well as the more expected stuffed domestic pets and wild birds, Potter amused himself by arranging tableaux of stuffed animals in human poses. As, for example, 'The Guinea Pigs' Cricket Match': 34 stuffed guinea pigs on their hindlegs, in human costume, playing cricket and preparing tea on a charming village green. Or 'The Kittens' Tea and Croquet Party' in which 37 new born kittens ape the appearance and habits of mid-nineteenth century provincial society. To this taxidermatic collection Potter added another: a random pseudo-scientific museum of curios, natural and man-made but with an emphasis on Nature's more grotesque errors. The museum has been kept together and is now appropriately housed in a Victorian mock-tudor town house in Arundel, near Brighton.

SOMETIMES SHE HATED Her. Hated Her with a passion that was pure and energetic. No good saying it was natural, normal, just a phase to hate one's own mother. That just showed their ignorance. If she were foolish enough to try and tell Her how much She was hated, She would say, 'Mandy, love, that's nothing to worry about. Lots of people think they hate their mothers, but you don't need to be frightened because I won't hate you back, and your hatred can't really hurt me. You'll get over it. I'm your mother, I'll love you whatever you do.' The ignorant self-confident bitch. She did not know. Did not know how strong and fierce hatred could be. Did not know how puny and vulnerable She really was.

And the hatred was real. As a matter of fact it was quite reasonable and well-founded. Look at Her now, for instance. Showing off. She was getting on for forty and it was time She learned better. She went on and on about sensitivity and respect, but She didn't have much for Her own daughter. Disgusting. In that bright red dress; fawning on him, like some animal. She did not always hate Her. Only when She deserved it. Sometimes everything was alright again. This morning they had walked in the Lanes while he had been at his conference. That had been nice, like a real mother-and-daughter. But now suddenly, she could see Her clearly: lumbering Herself up out of the car, placing Her hands gently, in a so-well-thought-out gesture either side of the belly mountain, to steady it. That was not necessary. It wasn't soft and wobbly like fat, but hard and firm. Tight. Full. Not what a person might expect. She was probably trying to draw attention to Herself again. Not very difficult: an ageing sow with a teenage daughter, nine months pregnant. It was obscene: all hush, hush and whisper about how it got in there in the first place, and now brandishing the consequences of that secret all over Sussex. She knew the secret though. She could find things out and guess and imagine and listen through the night. She wouldn't let her mother tell her though: when She had tried it had been easy enough to dodge, not to listen, to get away. There were limits. At school, though, in the biology class with that half-made thing bob-bob-bobbing in the formaldehyde (only a puppy though un-for-tune-ate-ly). OK. OK she wasn't such a fool as they all thought her. She knew things her own mother and Bill would never guess. OK she accepted that it was all normal and fine. But flaunting it in the public highways. Even Her breasts had gone huge and flabby with great purple tits on them. Her own mother, who had always been so slender, graceful, neat. Free. Free and not owned. And now She was all over him. Disgusting. People might think she was jealous of having a step-father: well they were wrong, she liked Bill. She was sorry for him actually. Though he'd be disposed of afterwards of course. Sucked in and destroyed. Oh yes. But for the moment he must be as embarrassed as she was. Though he didn't try to stop Her. He couldn't control Her, and he didn't even try. He deserved his embarrassment. Poor fool. Embarrassed, emasculated and disposed of afterwards. It had happened before.

They were supposed to be looking around Arundel Castle. Bill had escaped his conference for the afternoon and driven his wife and step-daughter over from Brighton. Now, after they had paid the car-park attendant, they discovered that the castle was closed.
    'O bugger.'

'O Mummy.'

'O Helen.'

Helen laughed, 'I've got a family of puritans.' She watched her daughter scowling and scuffing at the ground with her toe. It was bloody being thirteen, poor sweet. At least it didn't last too long. Poor little Mandy. Well, she'd grow out of it.

The wind caught the long crimson dress, drawing it back to outline her stomach. She smiled luxuriating in her sense of well-being and beloved-ness. Filled up with love. It had been too long. Now ... with a start she identified her own emotion: she felt smug. 'Let's walk,' she said.

Bill was worried about her; he wanted to ask her if she was alright, and he did not want to appear to fuss. She was thirty-eight years old; the baby was nearly due; she ought to have stayed at home, not rushing round Brighton Pavilian whooping with laughter. He could not help worrying.

She caught his glance and smiled at him, 'Walking is good exercise for the expectant mother,' she quoted. She pushed her arm affectionately but stubbornly through his and then reached with the other hand for Mandy. As she touched her daughter she felt a shock: Mandy did not pull away or even tense up, it was something more internal: but emphatically a physical rejection. She looked at the child but there was nothing in her face. Better let it go, not make demands, draw attention. Adolescence, poor pet.

They walked up the road with the river beside them and turned into the town. Helen walked in a contented dream, sleek and stuffed full with love. Anticipating too: when Mandy had been born it had been so exciting that through all the years she had been waiting to repeat the whole thing. And here she was again, older, more relaxed, more together. If it had been good then surely it would be better now. She looked at Bill: as the birth approached she was alarmed to find him blending in her mind, confusing, entangling with her first husband. The lovers in between were nothing; vanished. But Tommy and Bill: the fathers of her children. Different, of course they were different, very different. She was obsessed with this birth, pinning too much on it. It would come, it would go. She watched Mandy and Bill gently in the sunshine. She looked at where she was: Arundel, just here was a street of Victorian houses masquerading as something older. She liked that. And liked the sun warm on the back of her neck. She was glad she had cut her hair short. She liked that too.

Bill said, 'Hello, what's this?'

Mandy read out, ' "Potter's Museum of Curiosity" ', and then the opening times and the curator's name. Helen barely listened. Let them decide; she felt no preference about anything.
'Helen, do you fancy having a look in here?'
'Mmm, why not?'
'Hey, Bill, what is it?'
'I don't know, Mandy, we can but see.'
They went in.

It was all very well for Her. Stupid and dozy in the sun. She doesn't even care about Bill now, let alone Her own daughter. She had got what She wanted; taken it, sucked it in from Bill and now he could lump it. Couldn't the fat cow see that Bill was worried about Her. He probably didn't want Her stricken with labour pains in the public thoroughfare. She would probably enjoy that. Obviously She wanted everyone to notice Her and Her bloody boring pregnancy. Well, that would certainly work all right: blood and baby pumping out all over the street. Lying right there with Her legs held up in the air. That would be a laugh and serve Her right. But they'd probably send for an ambulance anyway, or something like that. But She might just try to be a little more considerate. Walking: she couldn't walk, waddling along like a drunk duck. One's mother out in public looking like a freak. People stared at Her, like a person with no legs or a grotesque scar — stare hard then turn away quick and pretend you didn't even see. Well her mother could grab her arm all She liked. She was not going to soften like her step-father; she was not going to be a crutch for some damn freak. She had better things to think about, the Selfish Bitch. God, how she hated Her and that bloody lump.

They plunged out of the sunshine into a dark passage. They emerged from it, part blinded, into a dim and tiny chamber. There was no space. Even the ceiling was hung with trailing objects not identified. The room was too small, and floor-to-ceiling, even in the middle of it there were cases and cabinets and loose items. They could not help looking. They could not distinguish.

17. Common English toads, eighteen of them enjoying a sunny afternoon in the park with swings and see-saws (mechanically driven). The very nature of the toad makes it difficult to stuff. In the olden days toads were thought to have venomous fangs and as a result were among the most maligned of creatures.

18. Dome of Australian birds. 19 & 20. Seagulls. 21. Kingfisher. 22. Pair of crested wrens. 23. Siamese pigs joined down the length of the body. The only malformation is the arrangement of the front legs, two of which are attached to the back and two of the four ears are joined together, often thought to be caused by witchcraft. 24. Small red-headed gouldens.

Out of the sun Helen felt herself wake up. She was amused by the quaint place: the darkness, the lack of space, the unscientific clusterings of the random displays, each clamouring for attention, each impossible to examine because of the demands of the others. She had a sudden stab of sexual excitement, and almost as quickly remembered why: the place awakened an old nostalgia for the long afternoons spent necking with Tommy behind the cases of tomahawks in the Pitt-Rivers museum. The memory of Oxford as always gave her a sweet taste. Since she had realised that she loved Bill and was going to marry him, all the evil thoughts that she had harboured against Tommy had disappeared as though by magic. Every memory of him was transformed over-night into joy. The bitterness had been obliterated so abruptly she had been shocked. Tommy her first husband had died at twenty-five. He woke up in the middle of the night; had said, 'Helen, I don't feel very well'; and had died. Mandy had been just two. He had betrayed her, seduced her and left her; a woman with a child and no husband. Left her with exhaustion and bitterness. Now she remembered him anew: nearly twenty years younger than Bill, young enough to be Bill's son. Tommy never got any older. She could remember him serenely. Tommy and Bill: the fathers of her children. Both of them had filled her up like this with life and love. Both, once they had done so, were somehow apologetic. And there was no real way to tell them how pleased she was; how she could take them into herself and make something new. Pregnancy was a gift from them to her, and she could accept it gratefully and make it her own. For her, this was the ultimate in physical pleasure — this growing from the inside and giving birth. Impossible to tell your lovers that their babies turn you on more than they do.

And the thought of the new baby excited her again and she revelled in the chaos and the enclosure of the museum. If there had been a spare inch she might have run or danced. Instead the excitement was directed at the museum itself; and she wanted to share it. 'Bill, Bill, do look. See this skull here, look it's got a great hole in it. Spear wound, poor bloke. No, wait, the catalogue says it's a woman. A noble Amazon?' Bill had already passed the case and could not easily turn round; his height was proving a disadvantage in these close quarters. He was afraid of banging into something, knocking something over, or off. He smiled back at Helen, but already she was not looking. She was calling to Mandy, 'Look Mandy, do look at this amazing little puppy, so tiny. What can it be? . . . what's the number? Here we are. O poor little thing, it was all wrong, premature, something like that. It only lived twenty-eight hours. How precise. Imagine wanting to stuff it. He must have been weird.'

O, she hated it. Out of the sunlight and into the dark. It was horrid. It was hard to see. She might bump into something horrible. She could not see what she was looking at until it was too late. Everything topsy-turvy and no room to make choices. Sick, horrible. The toads were repulsive, swing, swing, swing, daft, irritating, unnatural movement. One hundred years ago someone had gone down to a smelly swamp and killed them and opened them up and pulled out their real insides and stuffed them. And her mother liked it: She would. She had woken up now and was screeching round the place, as though life was just one big thrill. She would bump into a glass container and it would crack and all these dead things would come pouring out. But the little pigs. Bobbing like the biology-lab puppy in the preserving jar. But wrong, wrong. That was not what they had been shown at school: the two sealed into one wrong forever. They had been lied to. The tiny trotters, like something from a Beatrix Potter book, and the snouts palest pink and perfectly clean with the little bristles standing softly out, quivering, floating. Joined by witchcraft. The witch had struck them in the belly of the sow.

She hated her mother. Could one work such a mighty magic? If one touched the bloated belly of her mother it might burst. It would burst soon and out would pour blood and water and who knew what else. The skin was very tight, it was stretching. In the mornings last term after Bill had gone to work she had sat on her mother's bed and watched Her rub olive oil tenderly into the round smooth mountain. Sometimes her mother would seize her hand and force it down onto the stretched stomach to feel the kicking. Kicking, kicking, night and day. Attracting attention. Nowadays if she sat on the floor with her legs crossed she could catch her mother glancing nervously to see that the darkened triangle was hidden. She liked to catch her mother out like that; because She was the one who was flaunting Herself. She ought to be hidden away until She was normal again. Whether the piglings had one or two tails could not be seen. They were round at the back. But the gold-crested wrens were pretty. Once they had gone on holiday to Scotland: there had been gold-crests there nesting in the pine-trees. They had laid their eggs already and she had watched them each morning from her bedroom window. But the eggs had never hatched. In the middle the birds had got frightened or bored and had flown away. The ones here were caged, though, and still. Why couldn't She talk in a quieter voice? Her loud voice, Her laugh, Her chopped off hair, Her bright red dress, Her sticking out belly, were everywhere. She hated Her, she hated today, she hated the whole holiday. She wanted it to end so that she could escape and go back to school. The eyes of the puppy foetus at school were still sealed closed; it would never see. The Siamese piglets were the same; she could see their pale eyelashes too.

'Come on Mandy,' her mother called cheerfully, 'Don't gawp at those toads all afternoon. Aren't they clever though? Do come and look at this dolls' house. Far too much of everything. Very Victorian; isn't it just like Granny's? But they've really got the atmosphere right here. Look at this. O, come on. Bill's gone on already. Look, he's got tangled up in a stuffed ostrich or some-thing. He's trying to measure it. Typical. Come on, precious.' Mandy came slowly, not looking up. Helen put her arm over her daughter's shoulder, 'Happy Darling?' she asked.

'Yes, Mum.'

46. Lamb with two heads born at Wattle Castle Farm near Rye in 1887. 47. Kinkajou or Honey-bear from South America. Its long tail is used to great advantage when climbing trees; owing to its eyes being very sensitive to light it spends most of the day asleep. This particular animal had a particularly vicious nature. 48. Californian curiosities including a tarantula spider. 49. Java sparrow. 50. Blue Tit. 51. Stoat. 52. Above your head is a giant python's skin; a jaw bone of an ass; a street lamp, the only one in use in the village of Small Dole before paraffin lamps were used; a double freak calf's foot.

Helen walked after Bill. She could not be sure about Mandy.

Something puzzling was going on in there. But what could you do? If you ask someone if they're happy and they say 'yes', what else can you do but act as though you trusted and believed them? You had to respect that. Mandy could tell her, would tell her, if anything was the matter. They were particularly close.

'Bill', she called, 'Hang on a minute.'

'Tired, love?'

'O, don't bully me.'

'I'm not bullying, I'm asking. Afterwards we'll go and have tea in a shabby genteel tea room with cream and home-made cakes. There's absolutely bound to be one in a cathedral town. Mandy will like that.'

'Bill, she's not a child.'

'O, yes she is, but you won't recognise that. You're too open minded.'

'She's OK.'

'Darling of course. Look at this albatross,' he moved backwards and bent his head so that she could see across the narrow space, 'I reckon that it has at the very least a twelve foot wing span. Now *how* did they hang that round the neck of the foolhardy mariner?'

She smiled. 'I do love this place. He must have been an intellectually energetic man, to be interested in so many things. Mr. Potter I mean.'

'Well, I rather enjoy the curios. Detect here, Madam, No. 68 in your catalogue: one albino hawfinch, for God's sake. Impeccably taxidermed and a hundred years old. But these tableaux, yuck. Horrid little man. Poor rabbits, hardly born, their twitchy-nosed rabbit faces twisted into human likenesses, and they're made to knit. Even dead baby rabbits must have some rights.'

'Anthropomorphism.'

'OK and so what. Where's Mandy?'

'Ferretting about in the other room I think. I suspect her of lusting after the dolls' house and not liking to do so while we watch. You know, you were right, I am getting a bit tired and backachey. It's quite a weight.'

'Poor love, only a little while longer.

'A pram is heavier than this.'

'Ah, but I can help with a pram.'

'Bill, I love you.'

He stood behind her for a moment so that she could lean against him and rest her back. He admired the top of her smooth hair and the jaw of a shark which was poking within inches of his face, all seven rows of teeth exuberantly displayed.

Would a lamb with two heads be born dead? Would it breathe? Through which set of nostrils? When it fed, would its mother . . . ? No, surely it would have to be dead. It did not look new born, already springy, the eyes bright and alert. But glass of course, not sealed over like the piglings. Only one lamb, definitely, although two heads. What the hell went on in there that joined pigs, and two headed lambs crawled out into the light. Something dark and bloody. She had never told her mother that last term she had started the Curse. Watching Her belly fill up, she knew she was not going to tell Her how, all alone, the dark blood spewed out. She certainly did not want the embarrassment of her mother saying it was not a Curse, but menstruation, a women's thing, beautiful. She did not need to be lied to. It was so horrible that she did not speak of it to anyone. At night, in the dark, she stole her mother's equipment. Her mother wasn't going to miss these nine months. What came out of that hidden hole was filth and wrongness. She knew. How could her mother be so joyful, preening and prancing with that inside her? How could you know? It might have three heads. Did it bob there spitefully, waiting to shock and hurt? Her mother and Bill lying there in the darkness, and within the darkness what they had planted? It was their own fault. They thought they were in control but they weren't. The darkness was in control. Hauling Her grotesque body up those tiny stairs, too narrow for her hugeness. Her mother was more of a freak than anything in the museum. God how much she hated Her. The hatred gave her power. Her mother had turned away, forgotten her, taken up with that Bill, and now they had made something horrible together. They'd regret it. She could make them regret it. The pigs' ears had been joined by witchcraft. The power of hating. She could do that herself, because she knew about and believed in the darkness. The darkness made her strong. She could bind and blight in the darkness. And why not? She hated her mother, hated the baby.

230. Lamb with two bodies. 231. Marmoset from South America given to Potter by a sailor who had once visited the museum in 1888. 232. Duckling with three eyes, four legs, two beaks, four wings. 233. Dog with three eyes and two mouths. 234. Kitten with seven legs, two bodies and two tails (one leg on its back). 235. Kitten with four eyes, two faces and two

mouths. It was born at Broadwater, Worthing and lived several days. 236. Kitten with two bodies, eight legs and two tails. 237. Hat and shoes worn by Charles Wickham-Martin MP at Queen Victoria's Fancy Dress Ball in 1845.

No. No. No.

She didn't mean to scream, she didn't even want to scream. She was screaming; trying to scream, but she couldn't breathe. It was she, not her mother, who was the deformity. She had to get out, she had to breathe.

Upstairs Helen and Bill found themselves alone in a room. Slightly squashed between a glass display case in which twenty silk-clad kittens enacted a wedding ceremony complete with little prayer books and another cabinet in which two squirrels were having a duel-to-the-death, Helen leaned into Bill's arms. They were both excited. Bill could feel the baby pushing and pounding against his groin. He was aroused by her, by the baby, and perhaps most of all by the fact that there was no way whatsoever that he could relieve his desire here. They kissed.

They heard her screaming, 'Mummy, Mummy, Mummy.'

Bill said, 'It's Mandy.' Both of them were shocked by the panic they could hear. Helen pushed Bill gently and said, 'Go on.'

As he ran out of the room she noticed with shame her tiny spurt of annoyance that they could not even enjoy a simple kiss without interruption.

She blushed to think that she could think anything of the sort. As fast as she safely could, she hurried down the stairs towards her daughter.

She was the freak. Her mother, round and full, was the right shape. She was flat and wrong. She must be punished, not her darling mother, not her little baby brother. She must recall the darkness back into herself even if it killed her. They must not be hurt. She was sorry. Sorry, sorry. She had to get out. She blundered against things, her panic mounting. There was a giant shoe on the floor. There were strange things in the shadows. There was no space. She could not breathe, she was going to drown. They couldn't care less, they wanted her to die. No, she wanted to die, because she was bad. They loved her. She wanted to breathe. She couldn't. She knocked into another case, but did not look to see what might be in it. It was dark and there was not enough room. She found the little passage. She had to get out. She could hear Bill's concern behind her, but she must not turn back. She forced herself against some obstruction that she did not understand. It was the door. She pushed again against its implacable resistance, and then suddenly burst into the sunshine. After a second or two she began to breathe, painful blinding breaths. Then she started to cry, waiting for the arms of her mother to come down and hold her again.

Hyppolita

THE WAILING WAS high pitched, so that it seemed more like screaming, except that it was extended through time and varied in pitch. He had heard that noise only once before, briefly, after the battle in the Euxine, the day before he had challenged Hyppolita; that was how he knew, before they told him, that she was dead. He was so tired that the memories and the sound came into his head before the meaning did and its impact evaded him. (In fact it evaded him for four days, while he and the army came down again to Athens, and then on the fourth night it articulated itself in a lust so strong that he was angry with her: angry with her for coming up with him, and thus forcing him into private quarters, separating him from the young soldiers who could have relieved the lust.) The wailing and the memories, as opposed to their meaning, were continuous, and, before he was conscious of the knowledge, he had pushed away his guards and started to run, helmet strap flapping, towards the noise and the fact.

Hyppolita was dead. Also she had been mutilated: her breast had been slashed over and over again in what appeared to be a genuine attempt to obliterate it. He was sickened and furiously angry. At the same time he understood the savagery directed towards her sex; he had felt the same way when he had fought against the Amazons himself; the hatred of these powerful, alien soldiers. Unnatural was the easy word which indicated but did not explain the area from which the savagery and the anger sprang. He was also irritated by the insistence of all thirty of her women that they, they alone, had performed the mutilation, that it was the custom for their battle dead. He realised that this offended the sensibilities of his Athenians, and he also realised that it was not true. Again through his anger was an understanding, that they wanted to protect her still from the savagery and the hatred directed at her, and to protect themselves from the knowledge that it was directed at them too. Moreover they wanted to cover up their own failure; they and she had insisted that they should be her body guard and by this they were exposed as failing even to guard her body. He could understand that too but he was still irritated. When he had first known her she had worn her hair short like they did, but when he had made her queen of Athens she had grown it and allowed it to be arranged in the elaborate loops and curls which were the fashion. ('You don't have to,' he had told her, 'I will justify you before all Greece.' She had said, 'Don't be so pompous,' and later, 'So long as I give in over the little things like this I shall never need to move over the essentials. The inessentials are easy.' They had not been easy, but she had tried.) During the last five days, however, while she had been fighting she had drawn her hair down her back in a plain tight plait. Even the vanity that she had developed in her years with him was not allowed to interfere with her professionalism. Her women now presented him with this plait. Again a cause of irritation and understanding. He knew they had cut it because they resented it, and what it meant — her going over to his camp; they still saw him as the enemy, their marriage as her defeat. In her death they had wanted to make her more theirs, to palliate their loss. Once more the understanding did not overcome the anger; he liked her long hair, both because it was beautiful and because it was a symbol of her belonging to him, being in his camp. And beneath both the understanding and the anger was a resentment of the fuss; he was tired, other friends were dead, the enemy must be pursued, and now he was being burdened with this formality and the wailing. It was hysterical, it was feminine and it was out of place here.

For a while this balance of understanding and irritated resentment was the only emotion that he was capable of recognising. He lived with the combination and with his increasing tiredness through the next few days; the tiredness lent strength to the irritation and weakened the understanding. In the middle of the fourth night, as has been explained, he became suddenly and painfully aware of his loss and his resentment soared into a savage rage, first against her and his own weakness, then, seeking a rational outlet, against her mutilator. But even in this anger there was understanding, an awareness that she would have minded less about the mutilation than he did. She might even have been proud of it as proof that she had died in battle. Her confidence in herself as soldier had been somewhat sapped over the past few years; he had known this and it had been one of the reasons why he had forced down his fear for her when she had said that she was coming up to the war with him. This was another thing he had learned from her — that there were better ways of protecting people than keeping them alive. Also he recognised the irony, how the one breast had bothered him originally. It had given her a lop-sided appearance which had increased the feeling of strangeness he had had with her. Because of what he had been told about the Amazons as a child he had expected her to be grotesque, burned or very scarred, and instead there was the smooth flatness, the little undeveloped nipple like a child's and the small white scar surprisingly low down on her chest. She had explained about the operation, usually done before the girls reached puberty, the little slit underneath the girl's forming breasts and the glands cut neatly away. He had asked about the burning and the laceration of his nursery myth and she had laughed (she always laughed first and then explained seriously; not mixing the two herself, but letting the mixture remain with the memory of the explanation) and said that they would never have done so, that the time could not have been spared, that the loss of a fighting woman for that length of time would have been too dangerous. He had still been appalled, had tried to explain to her about exploitation, about his newly inaugurated laws in Athens, new civil liberties, new freedoms for citizens and protection for slaves. This had made her angry, she had told him that his new laws did not free men from military service, from providing weapons and tax money. 'It's just the same. Necessity. Do you understand? Everything you do to protect your state we do, only we have to go further, partly because we are women — physically speaking that's a real disadvantage and we know it — and partly because everyone in the world is our enemy, every army in the world hates us. No alliance, no rest. They want, they say, to "civilise" us, "free" us. A breast is a small price to pay to be free. Freedom to live as we want is a rigorous discipline, it always is. And when you want to live as no one else seems to it is even more so.' Pause, new voice, half amused, half proud, 'You know, a while ago they only did it to the girls who they thought would make good soldiers, not to the weak or deformed; then these had to live out their lives ashamed, marked out. There seemed no reason for that shame, there's enough without having it inflicted on you by your own friends; now I do it to all of them.' 'You do it?' 'Yes, it's a royal honour.' Then serious again, 'Freedom is a social thing, it must involve the whole society, the whole of it. You know that, to some

extent you try to articulate it in your own state, you must understand it in mine.' After this conversation he had found that the
breast no longer worried him, instead it confused him. He would
wake up in the middle of the night and reach for her, and feeling
the long smooth chest would think of Pirithous and murmur his
name until she woke up and took his hand and moved it across to
the other breast or down her long hard stomach. At first he would
be ashamed and turn away, blushing or sobbing or giggling. Later
she took away that shame and when it happened would roll over
on top of him, laughing and saying, 'Me, Theseus, Me, me, me. Are
you sorry?' When they met Pirithous again she had told him about
it laughing, and Theseus seeing his shocked face, had laughed as
well, and the laughter and the lateness and the drink had taken
them all to bed together and he had understood that freedom too.
After this he had loved her strange body both for itself and
because it seemed to explain her androgyny — a femininity with
which he could cope, which he did not have to fear, and a
masculinity without shame. When, sweating out the night, he
remembered some of this, his anger once again was muted; not
ended, but changed and mitigated. In the balance he felt neither
furious nor tolerant, but alone.

On the morning of the fourth day they were in sight of Athens
and the women and the children came out to meet the army and
he knew what he had lost. So he took Hyppolitus from his nurse
and led him to see Hyppolita. She had been cleaned and draped
and Theseus could not decide whether to show their son his
mother's mutilation. He did not because when he saw her her
deadness got through to him and he realised that he wanted to
cry and, at the same time, that he would never be able to cry
again. Men cannot cry in front of their women because they feel
that they must prove their strength, but she knew his strength as a
real thing because he had wrestled with her and won, so that he
did not need to demonstrate it any more. And because he had
humiliated her then, publicly, he had never felt the need to do
that again, to prove his own strength. After that he had given her
his private humiliation and she had looked at it and recognised it
and taken it away. There could be no more shame for either of
them. He knew then that he had had no right to his anger towards
her the night before; that she had come up to the battle because
she had needed her confidence, needed a belief in herself that she
could not take solely through him. But looking at her and holding
her son's hand, the wish to cry was stronger than either love or

understanding, and knowing that he could not cry, not there, nor ever again, was more than he could bear, and he bore it because there was nothing else to do with it. He thought suddenly that fighting the desire to cry was the hardest fight he had ever had, tougher even than when he had fought with her, and he remembered firstly her lying underneath him and knowing that she was beaten and still fighting, and secondly how much she had hated him. She had sworn at him with every word that she knew and the futile oaths had made her still more angry and he had seen the tears in her eyes and he had not let her off until she had begged for mercy, had surrendered audibly, the words forced out from her clenched teeth, and how he had laughed because he hated her and all the foul words he had ever heard had pounded in his head so that he wanted to kill her; he had used his hatred of her, his contempt for what he felt to be her perverse nature to block out his belief in his own perversion, his hatred of all women, his guilt, and the mess of his life. Ariadne screaming on Naxos and Helen rejecting the toys he offered her and crying until her brothers came and the language they had used on him and Minos waiting in Hell to judge him for his daughter's hysteria. After the fight was over and he had gone to bed, Hyppolita had come to his tent. (Years later he had said to her, 'Why did you come?' and she had said, 'I was so shamed that I could see no way out except self degradation. I wanted to sop my shame by total humiliation, self-inflicted to persuade myself I had some strength. Really perverse.' And by then he had been able to understand that.) He had asked then what she wanted and she had told him. He had said he was tired, she had laughed hoarsely. He had said he was drunk, she had laughed again and pointed out that there had been no drink. He had told her that she was deformed, that her body disgusted him, that she was perverse, grotesque, queer, an insult to her sex. His abuse could not touch her and there had been a sudden gleam of comprehension and triumph. She had jeered at him, pulled back his blanket, laughed at his body and its failure. Then he had begun to cry. He was tired and overwrought, and her mockery and his humiliation were more than he could stand; he would have twisted away from her but she took him in her arms and offered him her generosity. That was the one thing that he did not understand perfectly, her supreme, complete, generosity. When they were married his aunts all said that what a strong minded girl really wanted was a stronger man, that all women need to be dominated. The women accepted that she went to him as a prize of war, that having been conquered she had felt that she had no status. They were saying the same thing in different ways, but only she and he knew that their love was born solely out of their separate humiliations and her generosity. Later he had tried to offer an excuse for his impotence, had spoken of his mother and his childhood in Troezen; how she had taunted him to lift that damn stone, telling him that any man who was a man would be able to lift it, that if he wanted to be a prince he would have to lift it; taking him each day to struggle with the impossible even when he was only five or six; and at the same time being glad when he could not lift it, because then she could keep him at home and spin him tales about how his father was a god, how she was the beloved of Poseidon: a lonely deserted woman, with her warped fantasy life and no hold on reality outside of her son. He had never offered this explanation to anyone before but it had sounded pretty good when he had rehearsed it to himself. In the middle of telling it to Hyppolita however he had broken down. Its possible truth did not seem to matter, it was irrelevant. It faded like the nightmare of Ariadne's clinging incomprehension and the exciting, crazy, shameful lust that he had felt for the seven-year-old Helen: men were hung in Athens for interfering with children, but he had not wanted to hurt her, just take her away and give her presents and make her smile for him, for him alone. He began to forget these things; Hyppolita took away the guilt and gave him instead her broad humour and ready laugh, her body and her child.

Theseus looked down at Hyppolitus who was looking at his mother. Now that she had had her hair cut off they looked very alike, except that he was probably more beautiful; he had an Athenian fineness about his face that she had lacked. He had wanted her to have a daughter, although that would have disappointed Athens who wanted an heir. She had not seemed to mind however. The only time she had spoken about it, almost immediately after the birth, she had said, 'I'm so glad it's a son. Now I won't have to do it again.' He had asked her if it had hurt very much, she had laughed and said no (indeed her Athenian women had thought she was a witch, her labour had been so easy). He had asked her why she did not want more than one child, and she had explained that one was considered enough, that more than that was indulgence among officers in the army because of having to take the months off from training. 'But I would have to have given you a son, for Athens, you know. This seems like a perfect compromise. It's so difficult to mix the principles of two different people.' On the other hand she had taken very little interest in Hyppolitus, less than Theseus had. This had worried her some-times. 'I ought to care more. I know nothing about boys. I know nothing about children. They were never my business. I wasn't brought up to have them.' Sometimes he felt that pregnancy, like her hair, had been a sacrifice to him; she always made these sacrifices willingly and seldom let him know how hard they were for her. This was another reason that he had given in over the fighting, when she had said that she was coming up with him to battle. Her generosity seemed to breed generosity in him, a wave of understanding.

He stood there, looking at her, looking at Hyppolitus, remem-bering a little of all this and wanting to cry. The Amazons came back for some more lamenting; they had come back every day since the battle and wailed for hours. He remembered how casual they had been about the deaths of their fellows back in the Euxine. It had offended him almost, how they had left their dead unburied and unburned. She had tried to explain, 'Who laments your dead?' The women did. 'You see, we don't have time. When you have to fight as long and as hard as we do there is no time. That is why you must excuse our manners, our lack of art, of ritual tradition. You, I mean not you, but all of you want to take away our whole existence and replace it with something of your own. You can't do that, but you do the next best thing: you take away our time; we have none of our own, we have to give it all to you.' But now these same women were keeping up this incessant, high-pitched, irritating lamentation. He thought at first he had something to be proud of, that Athens and he had given them time and some allies, they were lamenting because that had nothing to do with that time, and without her those allies wanted nothing to do with them. That what he had given them was a further loss, he had taken them away from their own life and had not offered them an integration into a new one, a double aliena-tion, expressable only in terms of this impossible noise. But although he understood he could not stand the sound of them, so he took Hyppolitus and returned him to his nurse and went to his tent. And then despite his resolution, because he was tired out by trying to understand and because he had lost the source of his understanding, he began to cry. It was awkward crying without her shoulder, the tent post did not help and he stood screwed up and uncomfortable and irritated again.

That was not an easy day. The sorting out after battles never was easy. They brought him the lists of the dead and the ransom lists, and he signed them almost without looking. His loss was with him very closely, and because of it, because of her, he could not help realising how much the same victory and defeat were, how they were the same thing and how little either mattered: these silly wars with neighbouring states, petty humiliations where there should be unions: with her generosity, he kept thinking, with her generosity. His mind seemed to work properly suddenly, and he visualised a union of the Attic States. They were all so weak, so intent on the humiliation of each other to escape from their own humiliations that they none of them had any time. He wanted time, time to lament her himself and time to understand the generosity, the enormous giving quality of her love, that had set him free from himself, from his guilt. The generosity that had made her free herself. In the middle of these half-realised, unarticulated confusions he received a deputation from the Amazons; they came in naked with their chests bleeding and their eyes tired. One of them had been Hyppolita's lover; they were so like her and so unalike. The anger rose again. They wanted to take Hyppolita away to the hills and bury her themselves. 'But', he said, 'she is queen of Athens, they will want to bury her.' They said that she had been their queen first, that the Athenians did not love her, that they did. There was no answer to this one; he felt his fury rising. 'She is my wife, I want to bury her.' They were silent, ashamed because they saw him not as her lover, but as her conqueror. He saw their shame and understood it, but with his anger he bit into their humiliation, 'You don't even have funeral rites, you're a bunch of pagans. I want to bury her properly, because she's mine. Mine.' They did not answer for a while, still shamed, by his attitude and the truth of his words. Then the girl who had been Hyppolita's lover said, 'We can make a rite.' He said again, without reason, with anger, 'She's mine.' There was silence, they did not go away, they stood, lop-sided and graceful as he was used to seeing her stand. And then at last he had an understanding, an understanding of her generosity that would not own the people that it loved; an understanding of the fact that he could give them time to make something, just as she had given him time to make himself. And finally the understanding that the ownership of her body was irrelevant, they had the need, he had already ascended it. He said all this, they smiled, failed, he thought, to understand, and went out. He did not even think of asking them if he could go with them to their funeral. He was left without anger and with clarity. 'I have only to think of her,' he thought, 'I need never make a mistake again.' The thought contradicted sense, probability and his own knowledge of himself. He knew it did. He laughed aloud at himself; but the exultation was still with him and, delighted, he repeated himself, gaily and stubbornly.

Blessed are those who mourn

Then at his fated hour, Scyld the Brave departed to go into the keeping of the Lord. His loving friends carried him to the sea shore as he himself had asked. There at the landing place the ring-prowed vessel lay, the prince's ship, rimed with ice, but eager to start. They laid their beloved chieftain on the ship's bosum, glorious by the mast. They brought many valuable treasures, ornaments from distant lands. I have never heard of a ship more fairly fitted out with war weapons and battle raiment, swords and coats of mail. On his chest lay a mound of treasures which were to travel with him far out into the power of the sea. They also set a golden standard high above his head and then they let the sea bear him — gave him to the ocean.

I HAD A late 'spontaneous abortion' — miscarriage to most of us — at twenty weeks.

'By the twentieth week of pregnancy (measured from the first day of the last period, that is about fourteen days before conception) the foetus is clearly human. Its skin is no longer transparent and it is covered with fine downy hair over the whole body. The eye-lids are still fused but the internal organs are becoming mature. It is now about ten inches long and weighs about eleven ounces. It is very active in its weightless condition within the amniotic sac; and the mother will be feeling the movements within the uterus.'

Or: The embryonic group of unconfirmed, indefinable cells which I wanted to get rid of only a couple of months ago has become for me (for this is a subjective definition) my child; the child I had come to love and want.

That is my baby I am mourning and am not allowed to mourn.

'There's no need to feel guilty.' But what does need have to do with guilt? Of course I feel guilty. I never made her welcome, I did not treat her well. Perhaps she found her conditions unacceptable, perhaps she could not endure it in my womb. They are for ever telling us what lack of maternal love can do to a small child; how do they know that a foetus can't be affected in the same way? It's no use saying of course it can't: I know it can't, but how do I know, how can I be sure? That's what neurotic guilt is. What I do know is that I did not want her. Yes, her. I've seen her now, lying in my bread bowl. I rang the Doctor and said, 'Please, I'm bleeding, please do something. I'm bleeding heavily and sort of lumpily, I've got strange pains in the pit of my gut, please help me.'

And he said, 'O dear; look, go to bed, lie still. There's very little we can do. Either you will miscarry or you won't. I'll come round as soon as I can. If the pain gets very bad ring the hospital, otherwise you'll probably be happier at home. O yes, and keep the products of conception will you.'

'The what?'

' "The products of conception". That's what we call what you're losing, the blood and everything in it. We have to check them you see.'

What I think I'm losing is my baby; I do not say so though. The products of conception. A week ago I went to see him at the ante-natal clinic. He called her Mr. Bump. I felt that was nause-ating enough, but she was a person to him then, only a few days ago. He was telling me about some of the things she would be needing and how without a man-about-the-house he could ar-range for me and her to stay longer at the hospital, to give us a chance to get used to each other. But she was alive there. We were laughing together, the Doctor and I, because I said that her tiny fluttery movements inside tickled me. He told me how his daughter had kicked so hard that it tickled him in the night; he could feel her feet distinctly between his ribs. When I left he'd said, 'I'll see the two of you next month then.'

Now it was 'the products of conception' . . . at the beginning when I'd talked to him about abortion, or rather demanded that he should talk to me about abortion, he had not talked like he's doing now. He was a good liberal, of course, if I really wanted, he did understand, but he was not convinced. I might mourn after-wards, he did not like to use the word guilt, but grieving for what might have been was a very common syndrome, particularly from my Catholic background, if the need or the desire wasn't clear cut. Life was not impossible nowadays, not easy of course but a challenge, possible in my social position, assistance was available. My need and desire had not been clear, I'd felt grateful to him, he had understood that; it's easy enough not to be sure what would be the best thing, especially as he said, for us ex-Catholics, it hangs around that feeling, more than a feeling in my case, a definite desire, a sense of wrong. Illogical if you like, but I felt it. I decided then to be pregnant, to have the baby. What do decisions decide? I'd felt close to the Doctor then, but now . . .

'Perhaps, all things considered, it's the best thing that could have happened, in the long run.' He liked the long run, my nice liberal Doctor, that long run like the long range weather forecast, you can always change it, no one can hold it against you. In the long run, he had said, I think you might find having an abortion even more traumatic than carrying the baby to term; after that you could think about the future; successful motherhood means a surprising amount about how you feel about yourself, you identify, you know; you must take a gamble on yourself and your sex; a very satisfying experience in the long run. Well isobars drift off course, depressions and highs come and go. The Next Ice Age and a prolonged warmer period are both confidently predicted for Northern Europe, in the long run.

'Please,' I said to the telephone receiver, 'can we leave prophecy for a moment, please, my baby is dying. I know my baby is dying.'

'Take some of the valium I gave you for the morning sickness.'

'Doctor, my baby is falling out of me, she's going to die, I don't want her to die, not now, now I want her to live, I've wanted her to live for sometime now and she's dying. Doctor, please.'

I can feel him getting embarrassed; I can feel him remembering that he can't use his old palliatives, better luck next time, you can always have another, if the worst comes to the worst. I advise you to get pregnant again as soon as possible. You can't say those things to an unmarried mother. Poor Doctor. I can feel him shake his shoulders, long for a cup of coffee and long not to have to think what to say. 'Come on, you mustn't hang on here talking, I want you in bed, now. I'll be round as soon as possible.'

My feet are cold. The pain is bad, I agree, prepare to hang up. Then he said, 'Look, one thing, if you do miscarry, you mustn't feel guilty or inadequate. A single miscarriage, even at this late stage, is no *proof* of inadequacy, nothing wrong with you as a woman, if you see what I mean.'

I did not see what he meant. I had not even thought of it. I did not want assurance about my psychological welfare. I wanted him to do something to stop my child from dying.

With faces smeared with blood, breasts bared and garments rent the hired mourners groaned, wailed and recalled the virtues of the dead man. In his lengthy funeral procession servants carried cakes and flowers, pottery and stone vases, figurines and tools. A second group bore normal articles of furniture; and a third was responsible for personal effects like clothes and writing equipment. The sarcophagus itself was hidden beneath an elaborate cataflaque drawn by a pair of cows; it was mounted on a boat flanked by statues of Isis and Nephys, the boat itself being mounted on a sledge. The procession made its elaborate way, which included a ritual crossing of the Nile, to the tomb. The dead man's colleagues walked soberly, discussing their friend and his tastes and making standardised observations on the blows of fate and the brevity and uncertainty of human life. His wife made her prescribed formal laments. After much ritual activity, including censings, purifications, laments and the arrangement of immense quantities of equipment the dead man would need for his resuscitation and life in the next world, the priests and assistants were free to withdraw and the mason walled up the tomb's doorway. The friends and relatives however would gather in the tomb's lobby and eat and drink and sing before making their way back to the town as noisily as possible.

Afterwards the Doctor had the grace to say that he was sorry, so sorry, that if he had realised I was alone he would have done something about it, if he had realised how serious and heavy the bleeding was he would have acted more promptly, he would have done something. I do not blame him, if I had thought about it I too could have done something. There were plenty of friends I could have asked. I could not bear the thought of them: they might have grieved for her. So when she was born, miscarried, appeared, put in her brief appearance — I do not know the appropriate term — I was alone. I was glad though. If there had been anyone else there I could not have done what I did. I could not have spent time with her. Their embarrassment, and indeed my own would have prevented it. I would have had to have been strong and sensible and good and not put anyone out.

I could feel, quite distinctly, her being born; it was not in itself painful, and totally separate from the pain, the gripping pains in the womb itself. Probably she was too small, but right there I lost all faith I might have had in 'painless childbirth'; if my womb could hurt like this for her, so tiny and unresistant, what could it be like trying to expel a full-sized, real baby . . . or perhaps they want to be born, perhaps their participation makes it easier. I don't know. I'm avoiding the point: it seemed so right at the time; simple and necessary and good, I must trust that; already it seems strange and awkward and embarrassing. When she was ejected I was able, being alone, to pick her up, cradle her, not in my arms she was too small, but in my hands, examine, inspect her; discover she was not, as I had half-imagined an It but so clearly a She. Tiny but perfect, although skinny and wrinkled. A few beginning bits of hair on her head, but almost furry on her shoulders and back. You could see the blood vessels through her skin. Her eyes were shut. I wanted to force them open but it was not possible, they were sealed, no split at all between the lids. Her hands covered her face, I thought at first to stop me seeing her expression, but when I pushed them back I realised that she really had no expression, just a blank look, nearer to resignation, but not that. She had finger nails, they were transparent too and not fully grown, softer than my own.

My worst fear was that she might be alive and I would not know what to do about it. If she was though I did not have to detect it. I was as gentle with her as I knew how to be. But I had to look, I had to know. I slid her back into the bread bowl, after a while. The blood received her, she seemed to wiggle like a fish. In Mediaeval Europe scarlet was sometimes used as a mourning colour for the very great and important. Jesus washed us in his blood, but she drowned in mine. I don't understand why she should wait until I cared. I seems so fatuous, so deliberately cruel. If she was not set on living, why ever start, or why not give up earlier. So short a time ago she could have vanished and I would never even have missed her, never even known. Later she could have died and I would have been glad. Or would I? Perhaps I never got the abortion because I never wanted to; I could have overcome the obstacles, in this town, with the money accessible — I could even have asked her father. Perhaps if I'd had her aborted I would have felt just as bad. I don't believe that though, it is only just in the couple of weeks, if that, in the last few days that I believed in her, really believed that I was going to have her, that she was going to be my baby. Now I do believe and I do care; as soon as I begin to love her, she leaves me. The very stuff of romantic fiction, for this little fish-like person. I love you, how can you leave me, don't go, love me back, love me please; I don't understand, I don't understand.

Steady. Steady. Why doesn't the Doctor come? Why doesn't somebody come, please. I shall go mad. No, it's a perfectly normal reaction to miscarriage and especially late miscarriage, to feel both grief and guilt; and owing to hormonal factors, similar to those experienced after normal birth, these two feelings may develop into clinically treatable depression. So there, I'm perfectly normal. Or not, because my book goes on to say that it is of vital importance to talk over these feelings with your husband . . . well I can only hope that the book is wrong, unless they mean vital for him, because I haven't got one. At one point I even crawled to the telephone to ring her father. Darling, I could say, do you want to see your daughter? She's very beautiful though she can't look at you, and she's swimming in my bread bowl, the one you used to get such pleasure out of because seeing me kneading wholemeal loaves made me seem like a real woman to you. Well, now the bowl contains another mark of the real woman: the ability to conceive — alas, inadequately fulfilled, but you, better than most, know my difficulties in this direction. Also in the bowl, my dear, is some blood and some left over bits from what is meant to be one of the best designed life-support systems ever devised; which can support a human being for forty weeks in conditions exactly duplicating those in space, providing oxygen, nutrients and the disposal of waste products for the astronaut who floats freely in the weightless environment. This is better than male technology has managed to do so far. Unfortunately in this case the system has collapsed. Or, in other words, I have killed your child. The one you did not even know you had begotten. You would point out that male technology made fewer errors than women's natural systems; and inquire with earnest interest what the difference might be between male chauvinism and female chauvinism. These are the reasons why I did not ring him. I did not want him.

I was confused. I was not feeling so good. The pain was getting worse all the time, although I had supposed it would stop once she had come out. I didn't ring him, I don't think. I did telephone the Registrar of Births and Deaths. I had to talk to someone and it seemed as though one way or another it ought to be his business. It wasn't. I think he got worried while I was talking to him; he kept asking my name and address and if I was alone. I was worried too, because he did not seem able to help me. A foetus before the twenty-eighth week is no concern of his. It doesn't have to be registered with him in either of his capacities. It was never born so it can't have died. It has been born, I tried to explain, she is in my bread bowl, now, what shall I do with her? The law does not want to know if she died by accident, only if I killed her myself, deliberately. I don't understand, I said to the man on the telephone; I could not help it if he was sounding desperate. You haven't seen her, I told him, of course she has been born, she's a person, like a spaceman whose spaceship has broken down. I don't understand. I think he tried to explain. It's simple enough if I can remember it rightly: if I kill her, especially now she's getting big, it's abortion or foeticide, and the latter is a category of child murder. But if she dies of her own accord she never was a person in the first place. What is one to do? I felt bereft. The space between me and the world was beginning to be filled with baby, literally, physically, and it is suddenly empty and what was there, they say, never existed. Nothing, nothing.

> After the embalming her body was enclosed in a leaden wrapping, and laid in a coffin covered with a blue velvet pall. Her daughters and son came to pray beside her and attended Mass every day . . .
> The gentlemen of her household carried the coffin to the funeral car which was drawn by six black chargers draped with black velvet; a golden pall replaced her blue covering. The chief mourners were met by one hundred pensioners in black gowns and hoods carrying tapers, an ecclesiastical dignitary carrying a cross, and the bulk of the mourners.
>   The next morning two low Masses were said followed by the Solemn Requiem Mass in the afternoon. Then the coffin was lowered to its last resting place, the officers of the household broke their white staves and with great weeping and lamentation threw them into the grave. After that a funeral feast was provided for all the mourners.

I was brought up as a Roman Catholic. I have done nothing about this for a number of years, but it remains a part of me. It is quite possibly the reason why finally, despite indecisions, rationalisations, explanations, I did not have her aborted. The rites and rituals returned through the darkness and the pain. 'Hail Mary full of Grace, the Lord is with Thee, blessed art thou among women and blessed is the fruit of thy womb . . .' While the fruit of my womb lies bobbing gently in the bread bowl. Did she have these fears, or did the assurances she had received keep her safe from panic and fright. 'The desert shall blossom like a rose.' A few weeks ago my child was flower-like, an unspecified

grouping of cells with infinite potential. Already she is beginning to make up her mind; she should have inclined towards life
not death. Death is contaminating, it might prove infectious.
The Children of God, the Israelites knew: 'This is the law when a
man dies in a tent: everyone who comes into the tent and
everyone who is in the tent shall be unclean for seven days.
Everyone who in the field touches a man who is slain by a sword,
or a dead body, or the bone of a man or a grave shall be unclean.'
Our Lady, then, would never have prodded the foetus, she
would not even have touched the bread bowl, for that is my
daughter's grave. She will not get another. No grave, no monu-
ment, no memorial. Miscarried children cannot be given
Christian burial, they cannot be baptised. But she had a complete soul, that was why she had a right to live, why I was not
allowed to harm her. Is she to go to hell because I had a
congenital weakness of the cervix. She is innocent, innocent.
We must believe she was innocent; or did she want to die, did
she commit a moral suicide, suicide in the will? Did she have a
will? Deeds she certainly had, a whole biography. I have pro-
duced perhaps 180 ova in my life, one a month for fourteen
years, but hers was the only one to make the long journey, to be
impregnated, empowered, and break forth into generation. And
then what adventures she had endured: daily changes in her
conditions, both physical and mental, threatened with murder,
conspired against, surviving, finding love, cherished, and now
evicted from her home. I could not hurt her because God loved
her, and now I cannot even pray for her. There is nothing that
Mother Church can do for her; forget it, flush it away.

Holy Mother Church is embarrassed because I want to weep
for my daughter. The unwept tears clog our eyes. I know why
children cry when they're born: it is for all the crying they won't
be allowed to do later. Cry at birth before they have a chance to
say, 'don't cry, look on the bright side, don't think about it, trust
God.'

I was wrong it is not death but grief which is the infectious
disease; avoid it like the plague, it might creep out from between
the sealed eyelids and contaminate our silences, it might remind
us that we too will have to mourn, don't be morbid, don't talk
about it. I learned recently that ostriches don't really hide their
heads in the sand . . . but small children do something like that. I
have been watching small children lately. I saw a child, wearing
green shorts and no top; her shoulder bones like wings, so

delicate and mobile. She ran down the street and leaned against the wall, her face pressed to the bricks and shouted, 'Say, "Where's me?", say "Where's me?" ' And her obliging grown-up pretended it could not see the child, 'Where are you? Where are you?' Did the child really think it was hidden, or invisible, or was it a game?

I will bury her myself. I won't need a shroud because her nakedness is unashamed. Or, if sin is in the conception, she can use the red shroud she is lying in. And even now I catch myself thinking that I cannot spare the bread bowl, because nothing is simple for me anymore. I shall bury her in the back garden. I read somewhere that the stretched skin over the belly of a pregnant woman becomes permeable to light, so that the baby does not grow in the dark, but in a translucent dome, bathed in light. But I think my child is too young for that. She would prefer the quiet dark of a grave to the bright light of cremation. But as she has swum so freely and gracefully all her life, perhaps I should take their advice and flush her away. It is not for her, but for myself that I want some dignity, some humanity to adorn the process. You can buy a dignified burial space for your pet dog, but not for your foetal child. You cannot buy a gravestone for your loving sentiments. I could write her an epitaph: Here lies my daughter who grew in grace from embryo to foetus but died on account of her mother's laxity. No and no. I will not return to the guilt. I feel cold and tired. I wanted to want my baby, that is the best I can do. That will have to be her epitaph.

In the end the Doctor came of course. His hands were strong and firm, although his conversation was embarrassed. When I felt better and recovered from the loss of blood and the shock I was of course happy to learn that the Doctor had poured the products of my unfortunate conception into a plastic bag, and scrubbed out the bread bowl and left it to drain beside the sink, and carried the plastic bag off to the hospital incinerator.

To one's own dead one displayed extreme respect and care. As soon as the last hour was presumed to be approaching the dying person was put in a special hut, and when the spirit had departed the hut was burned down. Dressed in his best clothes the corpse was laid out for public view, which the survivors, with green wreaths on their heads, made deep gashes on their breasts and broke into long shouts of dismay, which alternated with dirges and speeches in honour of the dead. The corpse was wrapped in a mat and placed on a platform in the crowns of the trees. After the burial there was a big celebration, and food and other gifts were distributed to the sorrowing guests.

(The funeral rites described in the insets are i) Anglo Saxon; ii) Ancient Egyptian; iii) Mediaeval English; and iv) South West African contemporary.)

Conquistador

POWER, HE THOUGHT. Power and what to do with it. The flight from Spain useless, giving him only the power that previously other men had used against him. Finding no answers. How to turn power away from the act of commanding, mastering, dominating and yet lead these starving bastards, these loyal companions? They certainly had no desire for him to renounce power. They apologised to each other for him when he would not let them kill the native peoples.

Power, he thought. And then, food. Jesus Maria, he was hungry. They had, earlier in the journey, boiled their shoe leather for broth. Yet the Indians went shoeless and full. Food, and no more power. He wanted to get out of the boat, to go into the jungle and yield to it. The answer was there, in the jungle.

He had been filled with joy when they had left the icy mountains and the warm rain had embraced them: it rotted their equipment and blurred their vision, but the casting off of the old apparel and the steaming vagueness held a promise for him — the loss of the hard precision, the virile clarity that he had come to fear. The jungle was a new delight: the sun seldom penetrated the overhead roof of branches, but it was not needed. The profusion and fertility of the jungle generated a heat of its own: and they crawled through the humidity like a flea caught in the hairy chest of a man wearing a leather jacket. Around them they could hear but seldom see the signs of a dense animal life. Huge butterflies and flashes of parakeet moved across the green gloom. Used to forests where great stands of trees of a single variety created an orderly magnificence he was unprepared for this chaotic richness: palms and laurels and rubber trees and rosewood and mahogany and steelwood and bamboos and chocolate trees and silk-cottons and figs and acacias and purple-hearts and cow-trees and brazil-nut trees and garlic trees and cashews and balsa and more cedars than there were names for. Even, occasionally, the cinnamon trees for which they had come here, but never enough; never enough of anything to give a feeling of arrival. Occasionally giant hardwoods broke through the roof and towered away on their own, buttressed by flying roots like the great cathedrals of Europe, but living, growing, fighting for light. Not fighting, reaching: there was no competition. Even the dead trees stood upright, sustained by their comrades, and everything living supported something else. Creepers or great sprays of orchids six foot long burst flowering out of living wood sixty feet above his head. Richness and rottenness beyond imagining. In the evening the beauty was claustrophobic in its intensity; the sun slanting sideways broke up the monotony of green and revealed its variety, like a green fire. The heat and the safety and the darkness took him back to his childhood and when the hunger began he would turn in his sleep towards his nurse and there would be food and comfort, until he could not tell the warmth of his body from the warmth of hers and neither from the warmth of the jungle. Was that what he wanted? To cut back, with a machete of the mind, to somewhere before there was coldness and learning and authority, back to that warmth and unity.

But Pizzarro, his leader, brought the words and the fires and the lusts of destruction, down into the jungle with him. They cut a swathe wide enough for the two thousand hogs to waddle through. When Francisco realised that Pizzarro was ready and eager to kill, and worse than kill, to torture and maim every Indian he encountered, he knew that he would have to get away, escape, be free of this influence and noise. Volunteering to go ahead and forage was only an excuse. He and his companions had leapt into the small boat and fled deeper into the jungle.

He was in love again. A better, sweeter love than the pale shadow that had so driven him in his youth in Spain. He was in love now with the jungle which both freed and corrected him. He thought about power and hunger. He thought that they would all probably die here. They would anyway have to die somewhere. He loved the jungle and its peoples. Asked for no information they told no lies. Spoken to they replied, sometimes with a marvellous and wide generosity, sometimes with a kinship that he longed for. He could do no wrong: as he and the river became one all things became well, even his mistakes grew hilarious, tinged with the joyful fear of being tickled when a small boy. Once they landed in the realm of a strange feathered king, Aparia the Great, who had armies at his command, but also food and he

had given them the latter. Francisco struggled to talk to him.
Aparia asked who they were and he tried to explain: from Spain,
from the land of the Emperor of all the world. A land where they
worshipped one God. Christians: followers of a King without
power who died for them. Servants of a King with all Power, who
laid claim to all the world. Even while he was speaking he did not
know what he was saying, what he believed; he could not understand his own thoughts. Aparia could not understand them either.
Waiting, politely, until Francisco was finished he asked again,
'Who are you?' and again Francisco had tried to explain. It was
dark, sweaty, hot, humid. His brain was rotting like the jungle, he
had no control over his tongue or his mind. Again the King
listened, again was baffled and again asked 'Who are you?' Explo-
sively, Francisco lost his temper. There in the jungle, beside his
river he could stand it no longer. The hills of Quito, the highlands
he thought he had left behind him forever, seemed bright and
clear and strong and manly against the steaming confusion of the
river and the excessive piles of food. He threw up his hands in a
gesture of pride and cried, 'We are the Children of the Sun.'
Immediately he repented. What was there to boast of? Of killing
curious and beautiful people, like these, of raping women and
desecrating holy places. But the river, his mother and loving
corrected all things. Aparia was delighted, 'Brothers, brothers,' he
laughed, 'We too are children of the Sun, children of the Great
one, infants of the Sun.'

As they passed on down the river, fed by the generosity of
Aparia and for a while at least not hungry, Francisco was both
amused and ashamed. The river went on and on and did not
change, and perhaps it went on forever and would never bring
them to the sea. And beside it the jungle went on too, but not only
downwards beside them, but outwards, away from them also.
And no one could know how far, perhaps it too went on forever
and he did not know whether to be joyful or afraid. Was this what
he had come for?

The high hill country at Quito he had hated. The wind had
made his empty eye socket ache and the immensity of the sky had
made him feel blind. He had seen other men newly come up from
the coastal plain stretch their eyes and take in the enormity of the
space, but no matter how swiftly he had swivelled his neck he had
been fully aware that he was only seeing half of what the others
saw. Waiting up there for Pizzarro to prepare the expedition he
had taken to wearing an eye-patch which made him look rakish

and remembering his boyhood which made him feel cold. Much as he hated his cousin and commander he could hardly wait for the man to be ready. His desire to go into the jungle mounted and his anxiety increased with every delay. He asked himself if he was running away and knew that the answer was yes and that that was a good and brave thing. But of the wanting itself he was suspicious. He had wanted love once, very young, in Spain. She had been beautiful and good and witty — but he had persuaded her to become his mistress and after pleasuring himself on her caught for one moment, once only, a look of fear and disgust in her face so strong that he had put the whole ocean between them. He knew that pleasing himself he had hurt her, and that she would not blame him, that she was grateful to him for loving her. Not that power then, not that desire. In San Juan de Guayquil he had raped an Indian woman. He had not known it would be rape, he had paid her and thought her willing, but when he raised his face from her shoulder he had seen again that same look of pain and loss. He had wanted to be a conqueror: but recovering from the wound which cost him his eye and discovering how much he minded even that partial blindness and disfiguring, he thought of the death he had dealt out and felt ashamed. He had won a captaincy and lost his ambition. He did not know what to seek now except a loss of power, and a turning into himself to explore and use the power there. Men turned to religion he knew, but not that God, that barren violent God whose name he had learned at his nurse's knee but whose violence and power and cruelty he had learned out here in the New World from the Holy Fathers. Not that God, not that way. But something. The jungle called him, there was something to be sought in the jungle.

He knew well enough the dangers of penetrating a strange cruel land under the command of strange and equally cruel man. The jungle to the East of the great mountains and Pizzarro to the West of them had swallowed men up, killed them or worse. He knew, but also he had to go. He was restless at Quito all the time, impoverished and cold. He loathed the place.

He was happy when they rode out of the East gates of Quito on that bright February morning. Ah, a splendid sight: a Spanish army larger than the force that defeated the noble Incas, lavishly equipped, and handsomely led. Gonzalo Pizzarro the finest horseman in Peru, the most fearless and bold of all those fierce bold Pizzarro brothers, who could lead men to hell and bring back the few that he found worthy. His dashing kinsman and lieutenant,

Francisco da Orellana, who had lost an eye but won a province in the war against the Golden Indians. Two hundred and forty mounted Spaniards, the courage and promise of the New World. Four thousand bound Indians, and as many hogs and lamas, and then the great snarling pack of killer hounds, two thousand strong. Pizzarro swore by the hounds, 'Best provision we can have. Cheaper to feed than Indians and available for all purposes conceivable: hunting, fighting and even, if the worst comes to the worst, eating.' He did not need to add that they were handy also for his favourite activity, torture. Dogging wild Indians was the sport of the Spaniards; Pizzarro also did not mind dogging his own men if all else failed. His private motto was, 'If they have to die why shouldn't they amuse me in the process?' They had to die because he was Gonzalo Pizzarro. And knowing all this Francisco was still glad when they marched out of Quito and began the long descent into the jungle.

And now they floated down the river and he thought about power and food. Too much of the former and not enough of the latter. How to lose one and obtain the other. Desire simplified into something to fill the stomach. But that was not desire, that was need. Desire rose above that like a citadel and it kept them all alive. One night, trapped in the boat by the hostility of the local tribe whom he would not let them kill, without sleep or food for days, pinioned by the high cradle sides of the boat which were meant for protection against the poisoned arrows of the enemy but which served the mind as prison bars, the Companions had started talking. Who had started it he did not know, lost in his confusion between the sweet dreams of his good eye and the nightmares of his other hollow place; he heard only the vague beginnings, attending only when it became a game. It had of course to do with food — that humiliating and delightful obsession of them all.

'. . . and right now I would like roast fowl in French royal sauce.'

'No, no, wine from the valleys of Italy.'

'Seriously, what would you like best in all the world, not now, just now, but really. What is your great desire?' That must have been the friar, not the scribbling one who kept the account of the journey in the pretence that they would ever come out of the jungle, to the end of the river, alive; but the other who spoke seldom and then always of his God.

They went round the boat, cramped together in the darkness, too close to lie; a moment of the night lit only by the phosphoresence on the water, a moment of intimacy and honesty forced on them by the long river and the daily knowledge of death.

'Women.'

'Gold.'

'The thanks of the King Emperor, and his grant of land.'

'My mother.'

'A child.'

'Home.'

'The beatific vision.'

'To be able to read.'

'Captain?'

He had known his turn would come. His great desire? He could not name it because he did not know. To escape from all power, to float thus on the river for eternity. These were not answers.

'The Kingdom of Eldorado,' he said and the Companions cheered. Distant as dawn dreams and beyond imagining, that was why they were all here. The land where the Lord Prince covered his beautiful body only with a coating of gold dust and washed each evening in a pool of clear water which no one ever panned or sifted.

The friar said, 'I do not believe in the Kingdom of Eldorado. It's just a puny and worldly description of heaven; only a weak way of trying to say God and Salvation.'

They were silent in the boat; disappointed, disbelieving, shaken for a moment in the faith which had brought them all from Spain to Hell and now closed them in the boat, in the prison on their infant-cradle. But Francisco shook off his thoughts and asked, 'Brother, why are you here then?'

'There are souls to be won. A great conquest to be made for the Lord God.'

So it was just power again, power and mastery. 'They say,' he said carefully, 'I have heard there is a man in Spain, wounded in the service of the Emperor, who had turned to religion and has a way of prayer that is for the man himself. Goes inward to the heart, not outward for more souls. A way of penance and self-discipline, weeding out the desires, freeing a man to seek only God.'

'Yes. Yes, I have heard that too. A nobleman. Probably a Holy Man, but I cannot think it can be right – to seek something for the self, when there are so many lost souls, here and in the Islands. Not everyone can turn inwards, however great the treasure. I think it not so much a penance as an indulgence when there is so much paganism and idolatry to be conquered. These, all these, have to be saved. To the uttermost ends of the earth. Without elaborate retreats and mortifications I am safe in the arms of Mother Church, but all these savages are damned, eternally and forever damned unless we come to them and make them understand.

'Oh, it is you who have not understood anyway.' The other Friar, Carvajal, spoke. 'This man he's from the Basque region. The family of Loyala. I've read some of his writings. He's no man for turning inwards — he's a fighting man, he wants to form an army, a Godly army. His way of prayer is just exercises, drilling, military discipline, for the winning of souls. Don't you worry, he wants to exchange one sword for another, not hang up the sword of the Lord.'

Francisco lost interest. Not that way. The way of the sword. He had come to the end of that road. There had to be another way, a way of letting go, taking in not giving out; receiving, acquiescing, consenting. Seven hundred miles they had covered in the first eight days of their journey, when they had left Pizzarro and the main expeditionary force. He had thought then, I have let go, the river has taken me. Not a Conquistador now, but a twig on the river, giddy, dashed, powerless before the flow. I have let go, he had thought and he had been frightened. He had halted the wild enthusiastic rush of their first descent. He had wanted to assert himself against this mighty river trimmed with this immense jungle. He had needed to challenge the river, to prove himself a man, a noble man, Hidalgo, the conqueror of the Incas, the master of the river. 'Row back up-stream,' he had ordered the Companions — though then they had still been his men and he their master — 'row back up-stream, force the boat against the river, defeat her.' He would row back up-stream, rejoin his Commander-in-Chief, return to his power and authority, lieutenant to Gonzalo Pizzarro, the fiercest of the Pizzarro clan, the King Emperor's own Governor of the whole province of Quito, the slayer of pigs and idolators. Francisco thought he had rejected all that and escaped it, but before the power of the river he wanted to go back to what he knew. His courage failed him.

His darling Companions, the men he now loved and cherished and was loved by, had refused. Too aware of their own weakness they could not bear the thought that the river might defeat them. Aware too that they were better led now than if they returned to Pizzarro. They had a leader, a man of cool and established courage, a man of authority who at the same time was not likely to have them shot on a whim, or in a fit of temper, or with calculation to demonstrate his power. He was and he knew it not the common type of leader. And there was something else, frightened by the strength of the river and the darkness of the jungle, they turned their faces towards Spain, towards the ultimate source of authority and power, towards the motherland. Desperate, hungry and scared they groped Eastwards towards the morning, towards home. They refused to attempt to travel backwards up the river. Pizzarro would have shot them all; would have been willing to die alone and mad in the depths of the jungle rather than waive his right to command. Lost in his private struggle, Francisco had consented. They had gone on downstream.

And now he was not sorry. But joyous. His thoughts grew vaguer and faded away, except of course the thought of food. Around food and sleep the day revolved and they drifted down the endless river, rocked by its smooth movements, at one with its gentle force. Each bend revealed only another bend, and the jungle clung beside them like a mother holding her child by the hand. There were no orders to be given, none to be taken. He was happy and unafraid. The silence surged into his head and his bare toes curled joyfully as though tickled. He stopped even wearing his eye-patch, convinced that the empty socket could feel the damp warmth and the dark abundance like sight.

And so they came at last to the land of which Aparia the Great had warned them, for which the rumours and stories of their journey had prepared them. The land of the Great Mistress, the country of the Women Warriors. And here, for no apparent cause and with no hope of escape, they were mercilessly attacked by the local population. For seven days they could not sleep, they could not eat, they were driven and harried and killed and oppressed. Francisco was taken by surprise. He had come to believe that he alone was the oppressor, the only wielder of power, the rapist, the killer, the torturer. He had learned that they, the Spaniards, were the Conquerors: if they ceased to conquer, ceased to oppress, there would be no more violence. And that itself had been an assumption of power, a generosity dealt out to a weaker people. Now they were the victims and it made him furious. He had never been a victim before. He was angry and bitter and very much afraid. The old defences came back. Kill. Kill whatever threatens you, destroy whatever is different. If you turn the other cheek that too will be wounded.

Their boat was driven into a gully, against an island. He wanted to live, not die. The dream was ending. He was waking from a long dream and reality was returning. He saw the bright and polished courts of Spain, a civilised people, a people who must live and teach others. A people of great value, beloved of God, people who knew, who had a right, a duty to survive. He drew his sword and smiled at its preserved brightness. He yelled to his men, rallying them as they dithered like cowards. He was not afraid, his mind dazzling him with its great brightness. He organised the charge. It was the Feast Day of John the Baptist. 'Gloria in excelsis' he shouted and plunged in his sword. He felt it penetrate the naked flesh and he plunged and plunged and plunged.

It was the body of a woman. What he had sworn he would never do again, he had done. And on her face was the same look of disgusted surprise that he had seen on the face of his mistress in Spain, in the eyes of the prostitute in Guayaquil. The blood seeped out of her as out of them and what did it matter if the orifice was different. In his strength and fury he had practically hacked off her breast. In her spread out hand still her bow and at her otherwise naked thigh the belt that held her arrows. He had killed her.

After they had escaped and the Companions had calmed down he said, 'Who was she? Who was she?' They had taken captive an Indian trumpeter. 'Who was she?' he asked. And the man told him the tale of the Sisters: the women who lived in the dark interior and many provinces were subject to them. Their villages were built all of white stone and only women lived there. They could fight, but chose mainly not to: they took men as captives to have children by and if they were sons they returned them and the men to their own people, paying them for their services with green stones, precious and rare. They were beautiful strong and creative. They had much fine-worked gold and worshipped the Great Mistress, the Mother.

He had killed her. He had killed an Indian and a woman, because he had been afraid. He knew suddenly that he had killed his guide. Just as Pizzarro did, he had killed the one who could have led him to his own desire, led him through the dark interior and shown him the other God, the one who was not himself, like him grown large, but Other. And now there was no way.

The river carried them downwards — but now it was carrying him away and not towards. For a moment of sunshine and pride he had wasted his chance. He had known from the beginning that this was Their river, it was They for whom he had been seeking. And when the moment had come at last, after so long and sweet a preparation, he had thrown it away — he had driven himself into the body of a woman. That was not the right way. He was lost. Lost.

A short while after all this they noticed that the waters were becoming tidal. They were approaching the sea. They were emerging from the jungle and coming back to the bright openness of the ocean. They began to clean their faces, polish their armour and construct clothing for themselves. They started having to fight with the river. It had carried them generously for over four thousand miles: now the tide began to assert itself and they had to struggle against it — create sails and anchors and drag lines, the stuff of the ocean, the bright place which the white man had truly conquered.

His time had passed. Francisco led the activity, organised, ordered, accepted congratulations. He watched the tide coming in and going out as he wrestled with it with ingenuity and intelligence. He was heart broken but not without hope. Each time the tide went out, he thought, live, conquer, survive. And each time it poured back in he thought, return, I will come back, I will return.

But not this time. Not this time.

Francisco de Orellana, from Trujillo in Spain, was born about 1511. Nothing is known of his early life, but he must have left Europe as a very young man, for he had seen service in Nicaragua before he joined the Peruvian campaign under the Pizzarro brothers. He fought with distinction in the war, lost an eye and was rewarded with the Captaincy of the district of la Culata where he founded the city of San Juan de Guayaquil. In 1541 he set out under the command of Gonzalo Pizzarro on an expedition to search for the 'Land of Cinnamon' which was supposed to exist on the Eastern slopes of the Andes, and for the fabulous Kingdom of Eldorado. In the head waters of the Amazon the expedition became stranded for lack of food and a small expeditionary force under Orellana went downstream seeking for friendly Indians who were supposed to live there. Circumstances, about which there remains some confusion, prevented the return of this force and instead the small group in one open boat rowed on down the entire length of the Amazon river (previously undiscovered): an expedition which took well over a year.

Orellana was an imaginative and creative leader, with a number of qualities unusual for his time — not the least of which was his willingness to accept the advice and desires of his men. This factor may well have contributed to the comparatively low loss of life on the expedition. More distinctive still was his attitude to the native peoples whom he encountered: he had a remarkable gift of languages and proceeded always on the theory that live friends were better than dead enemies. This policy, until near the end of the journey was successful, and he was not only fed but fêted and befriended by Amazonian tribal peoples.

After leaving the river and sailing round into the Caribbean Orellana returned to Spain and immediately attempted to finance a new expedition to the land of his Amazon women warriors — after whom the river was named although they have never been seen by Europeans since then. Orellana's last expedition was a disaster from start to finish: shortage of money, rotten ships and virulent plague in Tenerife were just a few of his problems. Once arrived in the New World he failed even to find the main channel of the Amazon river and died in the delta in 1545.

The Dreams of the Papess Joan

THE POPE DID not sleep well last night.

She seldom does nowadays.

She did not sleep well and when she slept she dreamed, strange dreams.

The First Dream

First I dreamed that I was home in England, curled up in bed, with my sister Meggie, or with Peter; in the dream I could not tell which, but God knows I could hardly tell then, both were innocent sleeps and I was barely sixteen. Then my mother came in and I could hear her although the sleeping me in the dream was still asleep, and she said, 'Poor Joan, she's so sharp she'll cut herself. This will end in tears.' And when I woke up I was crying, so it was a true dream and I think it will be truer yet. If I had still been asleep I would have said to my mother, 'It didn't begin for tears, it began for a laugh.' But I woke up.

As I lay awake I thought of the other things that my mother had said. She had said the same things over and over again and we all thought them pretty stupid and most of them were. Another thing she had often said was 'Joan, you'll never get yourself a husband if you go on this way.' And that too was stupid but true. I've gone on 'that way' and I'll never get myself a husband, but I'm going to get myself a baby — I have a baby in my gut by a fat fingered cardinal, mummering and slobbering, making the word 'your Holiness' into the obscenest joke in Christendom; and the papal whiteness turned to red, the scarlet woman, the whore of the apocalypse; ah, mother, and the Holy Mother of God forgive me: pray for me as one woman for another and as the Mother of the Church for the Father of the Church. God knows, if I had wanted a baby I could have had Peter's with his sunny face and big laugh. I said to my mother 'I don't want a husband,' but she would smile knowingly. I said to Meggie 'I don't want a husband. I want to be a man.' And Meggie said, 'Why, Joan? They don't know ANYTHING. They can't do anything.' But I thought I wanted it just the same. I wanted to be anything I wasn't and I still do; now I am not Joan anymore and cannot find myself, I want, O how I want, to be Joan.

The Second Dream

When I fell asleep again I dreamed that my baby was born. She did not want to live. In this dream she was not born naked or anything, but already wrapped and painted like the Holy Child, gilt and blue and jewelled, and a tiny white face, like a small adult not like a baby. She lay quite still and did not want to start living and in the dream I kept saying, 'Breathe, baby, breathe' but she didn't, she wouldn't; she just lay there, quite still, and bejewelled. Even in the dream I thought that maybe she was right not to want to start living, because what can possibly become of her. I can no longer be a mother, because I am not a woman anymore, though I don't know what I am. But I did want her to live. I do want her to live.

Her father did not appear in the dream I am glad to say. He, the Cardinal, the man, the one who found out the truth, I will be damned before I will have him for the father of my child. Why I had him at all I don't know, I ask myself often. I ask myself if it was because he was the one person who knew the truth, and in his eyes the truth looked so lewd that lewdness was the only way to treat it? Was it perhaps a last desperate attempt to be myself again, to be a woman, to be what I really am? Or was it because I knew that I was No-one, that what he did could not matter, because he wasn't doing it to a real person. But he will have no part of this child. I will have no part of her either, I am not fit. God knows how it will work out, what will become of her; she does not even want to live. In the dream she was too perfect, and far, far away from me, so that when I said, 'Breathe baby; please live, please live' she did not even turn her eyes — but perhaps real babies do not turn their eyes either. I don't know, I have cut myself off from that knowledge, all I know are the scrubbed children, hushed and held up for my blessing, but the knowledge that I need, do they turn their eyes? do they smile soon? do they know? what do they know? these precious things are hidden from me, by me. Meggie probably has a lot of children by now, perhaps she has Peter's children with round, sunny faces. There was no sun on the face of my dream baby, perhaps there was moon-shine, but I don't think there was even that, there was no life at all. A child can only have the life its mother gives it and I have none to give.

I started on my adventure for truth with a lie. I set off down the road singing, but lying too. Sometimes I wonder if I had gone honestly, not in disguise, not in a lie, if I had gone to Leo as a girl and asked him to teach me, would he have, would it all have been different? There's no way now of knowing, but I do wonder. I could have told him, if not then, later; every time he called me 'little brother' there was the chance to say, 'sister, father'. But I didn't. Each time I didn't the next was harder, but I should have told him, if only for his own sake. On the Judgement day I will know fully what I refused to see then, what I try not to think about. He was worried, he was feeling for his little brother, what he did not want to feel and could not understand. Our lies don't hurt us alone, we do nothing alone.

And what will I do about my baby? When I woke up after that dream I lay awake and worried, worried about the baby and what will happen to her — without a mother, and without a father; she will have a mother who cannot, and no father, I will not offer her him as a father, he is a profanity. I wish I could send him on a mission to the wild Germans, or the Pagans beyond Vienna; I will be a David and set my Uriah in the forefront of the battle, not for his wife, but for his child, my child. I hate him. I don't dare though. He might speak, might tell me what he knows about the keeper of Peter's Keys. They are bound to guess soon though, people are so blind about the improbable. His Holiness is sick every morning, faints sometimes in the council, has started to put on weight, weeps when he blesses children, gives charity to poor mothers suddenly, although he never did until a few months ago; but they don't seem to guess. What will I do with the child? What will I do? What will I do?

The Third Dream

I went back to sleep worrying about this, and it did not make for sweeter dreams. I dreamed a simple, standard, horrible dream: that I was falling, falling further and further in and I could not stop. I know what it was too; I was falling away from myself. Outside was myself, was Joan, and I was falling away from her.

And it is all true. I started so casually, so innocently. I was so innocent that I thought one went to Athens to get learning. Athens in fact is full of pagans and the place to get learning now is nearer at hand, in France, at Aachen. But although it's nearer, by the time I got there I had left myself behind. Each time my life, 'I am brother John, a monk from England' was believed, I became less Joan; each time Brother John rose higher through learning and wit I became further from Joan. I cannot find myself anymore. Finally they said 'John, will you be Pope.' The answer is Volo or Non Volo. I could have said No. I could have said Friends you are mistaken, this is not for me. I could have said that without even telling the truth. But I was alight. I had come all the way, I thought I want to be Pope. I said Yes. I looked round to laugh with Joan, and she wasn't there. Only the Court, and in the Court the grubby Cardinal with his eyes suddenly widening. How did he see? Because he is a liar too? And all of that was in this dream although I was only falling.

'I want to be a man,' cried the child Joan; and Meggie had said, 'Why Joan? A woman can do anything, can carry the Christ; a man can give nothing, only get.' But Joan would not see it, preferred lying, was too stupid to see where it would land her, dressed up in a monk's habit and set off laughing down the road to Athens. Meggie said, 'But Joan, women can be saints.' Joan didn't want to be a saint. 'But Joan, women can be rulers.' Joan didn't want to be a ruler. 'But Joan, women can be scholars.' Joan didn't want to be a scholar. When Meggie sang the Magnificat, Joan didn't want to be a poet. She wanted to be a man. 'But why, Joan, why?' and Why, Joan, Why, I ask myself, but I cannot ask Joan anymore because she does not exist; I have come too far and there is no way back. 'It's only for a laugh, Meggie, for a joke.' And the greasy Cardinal found it a joke, a joke to sully the world, and God forgive me, the cross too. With his dirty fingers, prying, groping, he found it a joke. 'You were both conceived in laughter,' my mother would say when she was drunk, it was not a platitude, it was the one thing she would say without making us angry. We had no father, fathers, we were fathered by a laugh. Well, mother, my child was conceived in laughter too, but not sunny laughter, not my laughter, but the laughter of a lecher; 'His fucking holiness,' he tittered, driving a sword into me and into the heart of the church, the body of Christ. I have not wounded myself alone. Indeed I have not wounded myself the most, but the church, the nailed body of Christ.

In the dream I fell further and further and woke up calling not for mother or lover, but for myself. Joan, Joan, Joan, and there was no answer. What the papal guards must have thought would be better than the truth. I swear to God I leapt up after that dream to call for my confessor, but I never did. John VIII has nothing to confess; so help me; as Pope I have been good, renowned particularly for learning, for compassion and for simple good sense, a little greedy for power perhaps, but sound, theologically and strategically. And how can little Joan from England call up the papal confessor in the small hours of the night, and even if she did what could she say? How can I confess to a man? Our Lady went not to a man but to Elizabeth, to comfort and be comforted.

The Fourth Dream

But perhaps the thought of confessing soothed me, because I slept better after that and when I dreamed it was a gentle dream; I dreamed of the convent. There was a stream, some cows and some nuns. I think it was in England. A set of small cells, but not for hermiting — for working, and praying, and being together. In the dream there was an abbess, looking a bit like Leo but without the silly droop in the nose, and with a gentler ambition, not to go to Rome, but to stay still and build up. When I woke, I tried to think that the life seemed little and boring, but I cannot think so in my heart. I think too that I could be useful to a community like that, because of my learning and knowledge, and they could be useful to me. At first I thought sadly, 'I wish I could go and be with them,' and then I realised that I could. When the time comes that I cannot hide about the baby anymore, I will simply go away — I would like to think that I could go in truth, but I have lived too long with lies and I cannot go back to the truth now, not here. I will go away and have my daughter and take her to England, and I will find Meggie and give her the baby, and then I will go to the convent, among women, and start to learn again, start to try and find myself. I ought to go now, today, I thought in the early morning; the pope-self demands his time, but I shall go soon. I don't trust Pope John, he is a liar, but I can trust the baby, the baby will force me to go. Soon, I hope, I should like to go home.

*   *   *   *

The Last Dream

It was a dream. She never went home to her convent. She mis-carried a son during a papal procession and was stoned to death, as an anti-Christ, by the crowd.

The Papess Joan, as John VIII, is said to have held the pontifical office from 853 to 855 A.D. In 1601 she was anathematised and declared never to have existed. That both should be necessary shows the con-fusion the Church felt about even the possibility of a female intruder.

No way out but through

EVEN IN THE desert there are cacti. The Bedu survived and so had she. Even in the desert there is beyond the desert. Not a mirage, a reality. She had arrived there. Unlikely though it had seemed, she had survived. He could not kill her. He had tried and failed. She was not afraid of him anymore.

It was the middle of the night and she lay in bed waiting for him: warm, comfortable, at home, unafraid. Alive, actually alive and only a little bit nervous. She remembered, almost giggling at the contrast, standing in the restaurant's pink tiled ladies' loo and vomiting. Vomiting him up, throwing out him and eight years with him. 'You're late,' he had said. She'd apologised, muttering feebly about baby-sitters... hard to find them at two hours' notice... Paul's kindergarten teacher, with her sunny smiles and her really-it's-no-trouble-at-alls... and it was a trouble making coffee, tidying the house, apologising for the mess... no time to wash her hair... she looked horrible... 'Your hem's coming down,' he had said and she had apologised and giggled coyly, trying to get him to laugh at her, to be cheerful, but he had looked cross and shamefaced, but of course, 'your hem is coming down' and 'I want a divorce.'

She had given him the divorce. Her way. A hard frigid woman. 'Do it my way, James,' she had said, forgetting to apologise, 'and we'll do it quick. Otherwise, I won't consent. You have nothing, nothing against me and I won't consent. It will take you five years. Five years Jimmo,' even at this moment the absurd intimacy of habit, 'you'll be nearly forty, you'll be fat. Is she going to wait five years? I'll give you a divorce. On a plate. I won't ask for mainte-nance; you get the house, you get the savings, you get the lot and you get the kids.' He was furious. His neck swelled and he had not looked very lovable. He had cried out in pain almost, 'It's spite, pure spite.' And she had said, 'I don't care.' It wasn't true. She did care; one more time her heart was wrung for him; one more time she had nearly offered herself, from habit, from training and from tenderness, as his sacrificial lamb. Nearly, not quite. It had been his idea, almost. 'The kids will love her,' he had said. The callousness had shocked her into some sort of life. 'Good,' she had tried to be calm, 'because she is going to have to look after them.' 'It's spite,' he said over and over again. She wanted to say you are boring me but she had not trusted herself. She had had to embrace her hatred for him. Only hating him could she be safe, safe from him and safe from herself. She hugged her disgust like a lover and found some strength there. Hating him not because he had been unfaithful, not because he no longer loved her, but because he was oblivious of her, prepared to make her suffer, to kill her, starve her of herself, of her space and time and personality, just to replace her like a car with a newer, sexier model.

She had fought him off. But only just. Now she could remember almost smugly how she had defeated him and herself and remade herself, a real life out of the wreckage. Now. Then it had been hard, really hard to conquer the habits of service. She had forced herself, 'You'll have to keep the children,' confining herself to necessary facts, while her heart bled, not for them — four tough nuts — but for him. She was being mean to him. She wasn't doing things the way she wanted. She wasn't being a real woman. She had felt guilty. I have to stay alive she had yelled silently at her softening self — and she had groped her way to the Ladies and been sick. Throwing up for what seemed, even in retrospect, to have been hours, discarding with anguish her love, her children, and eight years of her life: the price of survival. And then she had gone back to eat dinner with her would-be murderer. Anything I do, she instructed herself with as much firmness as she could manage, is self-defence. Even if she killed him, killed his newfound love, and his mighty self-esteem, it would be justifiable self-defence. She had a right, a basic right, to stay alive. To him she had said calmly, refusing to be drawn into any more discussion, 'I will have to look for a job of course. Could you give me a month? I'll move out after that whatever happens. I will see a solicitor tomorrow and start proceedings for divorce on grounds of adultery with whatever her name is. Could you just jot down the details for me?'

Memories lead oddly, with great blanks and startling clarities. Where were the children at that time? Now that she knew them so spaciously they moved in and out of her daily thoughts without effort, with grace and pleasure. Had she not cared for them that much if they appeared so little in her memories? Or had she suppressed them along with her guilt about them? Silly. They had come by no harm, there was nothing to be guilty about. But then James, and not alone, had done his best to make her feel guilty about them, and had succeeded. She remembered nothing about them from that year at all. Her solicitor though, she could remember definitely. It had all been strange with her man-of-law. They had not understood each other very well. He had thought that she was either mad or concealing something awful and he was curious to know what. She had found it difficult to say the necessary things which seemed to her to have no bearing on the truth although they were the facts. Adultery, the scarlet letter — no that was women — but the greatest offence. Adultery, infidelity, sex, those things weren't crimes: if she had had his opportunities who knows what she might have done — but she did know and she would not have done them. But attempted murder, that is a crime. Cruelty is a crime, is Grounds. But how does one say to the lawyer, a friend of the family moreover, 'My husband, in my opinion, has tried to kill me.' What could the lawyer say, 'How Caroline? On what day? Where? With What?' Like the game the children played. Cluedo. Miss Scarlet, in the drawing room, with the lead piping. No, no, Mr Lawyer, not like that, but slowly over the years. He has tried to kill me with sensory deprivation, intellectual starvation, belittlement and lack of interest. And now that I am very weak, indeed it is questionable if I am alive at all, he wants to turn me loose with too many children and not enough money, a burden no woman can carry alone, let alone one weakened as I have been, by dependency, child-bearing and the nuclear family.

No, obviously, she could not say all that to the lawyer, and she had not said it. She had said, 'My husband, the man I love,' — and ah, there was the rub, she did love him — 'has committed adultery with a hotel receptionist and I want to divorce him. He will not contest it.' He wanted the divorce; she dared not contest it. Justice was so blind that the poor truth was mangled and finally lost, like her, in the ramification of facts and processes. 'I am not seeking maintenance. He will have full custody of the children. I will not contest it.' Will not, cannot. The instinct for self-survival is so strong that women rush from burning houses leaving their beloved babies to roast and afterwards go mad with the knowledge. She had not gone mad, she had gone sane. She did have a right to stay alive. She had not bothered to try and explain to the solicitor. And he had said, 'But Caroline . . .' and he had kept on saying it.

'But Caroline, James is the guilty party . . .' 'But Caroline, of course you can have the children, no judge would dream . . .' 'But Caroline you could claim maintenance.' But Caroline the children . . . motherhood . . . maternal rights . . . maternal deprivation . . . innocence . . . guilt . . . But Caroline . . . And how could she insert into that energetic lecture the fact that she didn't want his lousy money, or any other part of him, even his children, that she wanted to be shot of him, to get him off her back, to spew him out of her life. That she wanted, simply, to stay alive. That she had qualifications, skills, rusty but real; that behind this weakness, behind this crumbling facade she was an able-bodied woman. She was a person and could keep herself, but not if she had the children. They were excess luggage that she couldn't carry. That James and his new wife and the solicitor and all the other people who told her what she ought to do and how she ought to behave did not know that children could kill; they could be dead weight. They would have to learn. She had a right to stay alive. But she had not needed to say any of those things. Adultery made her magically innocent: she set the terms, called the tune, named the price. She liked that. But she didn't understand. She was grateful but baffled: five minutes in the back of a car, against a wall, in a bed, a matter of less than inches would let one off those irrevocable vows, while murder, discreetly practised, would not. She had not had to explain, she had only had to hold on: against the lawyers' Rights and Justice; against her acquaintances' sentiments; against James' pain and anger; against the children's bed wetting and withdrawal. Hold on to the fact that her need was as great as theirs; that all men were born equal and under English law that technically included her.

And so. So here she was in the middle of the night, waiting for James and alive. Definitely alive and even healthy and strong. She had made it, she was a survivor. It hadn't been easy: only when she had actually had to try had she realised how little remained of her as a person. The impulse to live, to grow and be was practically gone; the energy required to free herself from herself was almost more than she had. Almost, not quite. She thought that she had worked hard and had won, thanks to friends and luck and social circumstances. She had set her sights low too, had accepted that she was crippled, limited; that there were old delights that would never return, scar tissue that would always show. But she had found new pleasures, new patterns. She had set herself objectives, disciplines, treatments. She had worked. Not easy, but she was alive, tough, and (when in a courageous mood) even happy. So why was she nervous? She reprimanded herself firmly. Because she knew why James was coming. Because his marriage was falling apart under the strains she had imposed on it. And she was not free of it, of them and she never would be. Because of James, because of herself, because of the children every contour of that marriage was of concern to her, and she had to face that fact. Her smooth dispassionate life was dependent on two people she could not trust: dependent on a man she had no right to love, a man who had tried to kill her. Dependent on a fluffy blonde, even more a victim than she had ever been. At first she had not acknowledged, had not even recognised that dependence; but as she fell in love with her children again she had been forced to know how she stood. When she learned from them that their father's marriage was in danger there was no escape. She had earned her life, her dignified peace, through a trick, and in the best theatrical traditions it was going to catch up with her. She had consciously, even conscientiously, made their lives impossible for them, and because she had been successful she was now going to fail. If his wife left him how could things be the same, how could she leave James alone, how live with the devoted cringing part of herself which she had given him over ten years' ago and was his till death if she could not say to it, every morning, 'That is a married man, some other woman's man, don't do to her what was done to you'?

This loving him still and always had been the most difficult part of her new life. It was humiliating, nauseating. When she had at last comprehended that James had been 'unfaithful' to her she had thought with some glee that now she would take lovers. Have fun, casually, erotically. She had found the idea pleasurable, but when opportunities presented themselves in practical forms she had found, to her annoyance, that she was not interested. She decided that she had lost the knack; that she was a victim of the Victorian double morality; that she was naturally undersexed; that he had reduced her to frigidity. But no, she had been forced to admit that she loved him. That is ridiculous, he tried to kill you, he didn't even know he hadn't succeeded, it is obsessive, it is silly, she would shout at that constantly loving self, like a nanny who had caught a child kissing a dirty stray dog. But no, wept that self once she had located and learned to hear it, he didn't know what he was doing. He thought I liked it. It was your fault, you let yourself in for it, you let it happen, it was your fault, you didn't stay alive for him, you consented. The solicitor had said, 'You must not sleep with him again, you must not sleep in the same house with him, or let him in your bed; you must not seem to condone his adultery, to consent.' But the part of her that loved him, that longed to die for him, that yearned to be killed so long as it was by his hand, that part of her that consented, daily consented to his adultery would not consent to hers. And so that this sneaky despicable self would not get out of hand, would not reduce her to whimpering and begging, she allowed it some space in her life. She didn't even try to love anyone else physically. She stayed chaste. She had herself under control. But time did not kill her love, which refused to die. It was as tough as she was. It made her nervous.

She knew that if she could only stop loving him the other problems would vanish too. Sometimes when people asked, with a slightly salacious curiosity, why James had the custody of the children, she would have to stop herself from crying out, 'Because I'm not fit, not worthy to be a wife or a mother; my husband judged me inadequate, so obviously I cannot show myself to be a proper woman.' She schooled herself to a more acceptable lie, to say, 'He was getting re-married, it seemed more convenient, more stable for them, we simply chose this way.' And of course it was not true, she had not chosen simply, there were no simple choices. But then why did that part of her agree with James that it had been 'spite, pure spite.' I was dying she cried again, and the children in innocence would have finished me off. He, not me, he broke the contract, he was guilty, he was unfaithful — 'unprovoked infidelity' the judge had said, his not mine. And she was growing more convinced, of course she was getting better. It was bound to take time, to relearn the responses he had taught her. She was getting stronger, more free of him. She was more able, more capable; now at last she was beginning to love the children. She was beginning to take a delight in them, in having them camped about her tiny flat, curled up warm and naked, their moving flesh against hers in her narrow bed, hugging her graspingly, swinging their legs, filling their space, being her children. Then James had rung her in the middle of the night, waking her from a good sleep, asking if he could come round, now, and talk to her. She had been able to say, 'Yes of course, come on round', with outward calmness, and without fear.

She was lucky. Slow at realising what happened to her, it was not till afterwards that she knew how lucky she had been, that this crisis had come in the middle of the night. The bell rang before she was even fully awake and she stumbled warmly to the door. He said, 'She's left me. Marilyn's left me.' If she had been more awake and crisply dressed she would have said, coolly, 'And what is that to me?' but she was too warm, too sleepy and too naked under her dressing-gown to lie to him. Because he looked so like a sad, fat little boy, so like their son, she said instead, 'O, my poor lamb, come in.' He came in, too big and strange in the tiny flat. He looked out of the window and said, 'Caro, I want her back, whatever shall I do?' She looked at the balding back of his head and saw for the first time that he really loved his wife. That James, her man, her Jimmo, the father of her children, her once and only lover, was in love with another woman. And with a smile she struck a deft and final blow at that part of herself that loved him and wanted him back; she said, 'I'll take the children.'

He did not understand. She said more slowly, the doubts creeping in, 'I'll take the children, I mean properly, permanently.' She paused again, then, 'It was too much to do to her. It was spiteful. It was a mean thing to do. Mean to you and her, to them too probably. It's my turn. We can try taking some of the weight off her poor shoulders.' She saw all the old traps: washing and feeding and paying and listening; being available at all times to other human beings; and this time there would be her job and her aloneness. But she was learning to love them now and they were older and she was stronger and she would not let them, quite simply she would not allow them to destroy her.

And James on whom she had expended so much love, for whom she was giving up so much, said, 'God damn it Caroline, if you'll have them now what have we been waiting for all this time?' He did not, could not see her as a person, could not see that she was stronger and better now than he had ever known her. That being without him was good for her, and she was different, changed. She felt strange, joyous; by my sacrifices, sang her heart, I am free of him, free of him forever, he cannot hold me nervous on his chain anymore, never again. I am free of his insinuating murderous hands. I'm alive. Death hath no more dominion, she sang as she offered him coffee. Her mind was wrestling already with the details of stretching salaries and finding schools and working out how much money she would ask him for, and somewhere far away there was a tiny loneliness, but she knew that the easy life of yesterday had been a mirage. Now she was truly out of the desert, at the oasis of fresh water. She was not just alive, she was free.

He did not know. That would be too much to expect. He could not understand that she had so shattered her elegant life for him that she was free of him forever. He had invented the terms of their new relationship in a hotel room three years ago; he held to that, she acted always from spite. He eyed her with sulky irritation. When he was ready to leave he said, 'If she won't come back it will be your fault. I will kill you. I'll come round here and kill you.' But she only smiled. He had tried for years to kill her and he had failed. How could he hope to kill her now. She had cut through her chains and he would never again get anywhere near her. She told him to hurry up and get moving and her tone was almost maternal.

Lilith

In the beginning was the Word and the Word was
with God and the Word was God. And all things
were made by him and without him was not
anything that was made. In him was life.

And in the beginning God created heaven and earth.
And God saw that it was good.
God created man in his own image, in the image
of God created he him, male and female
created he them.
And behold, it was very good.

but later, after many things, and for many reasons,
The Lord God caused a deep sleep to fall upon Adam
and he slept; and he took one of his ribs and
he closed up the flesh instead thereof. And
the rib, which the Lord God had taken from
man, made he a woman, and he brought her unto
the Man. And Adam said, This is now flesh
of my flesh and bone of my bone: she shall be
called Woman because she was taken out of Man.

CAIN, SON OF Adam, laughed only once during all the years that he
spent out in the Land of Nod. He did not have much to laugh
about. The mark of God was upon him; an open sore, always
putrid, into which his long hair was always falling. He was an
outcast. He was completely alone. He had killed his brother and
had been banished, to protect him from vengeance, and protect
those who might have wanted vengeance. Sometimes he thought
that he might even like vengeance; it would come as a relief.
There was no relief. He was alone. But he did laugh once.
Lilith, daughter of God, made in his image and pure in her
substance, free and unfallen in her nature and fettered by her

desire, was sleeping under an aloe tree when Cain came upon her. Her home was in the Red Sea, under the coast of Egypt, but she left it often, seeking for herself. Asleep she looked smaller than in fact she was, but even so she looked like nothing that Cain had ever seen, known or dreamed of. She was made, like Adam, in the image of God, but in an image that has not since been realised even mentally. The Image of God the Feminine. When she had chosen to go away and search for herself in the lonely places, when she had chosen to leave Adam, he had gone to God — frightened, angry and lonely — with the request for a new spouse, and with a request that that Image of God would be hidden for ever from the imagination of man. In those days God had been gentle in all things, except the act of Creation, and he had consented, though sadly because he had not wished to be hidden in any way from his people and his friends. He had granted Adam's wish, but had shown him that even he, God, could not keep knowledge from those that sought it faithfully. Adam himself must be the guardian of the secret image.

Adam was made in the image of God, and Eve was made, by God, at Adam's request, in the image of Adam's dreams. Now we see through a glass darkly.

When Cain approached her, Lilith woke up. She opened her eyes and smiled. Lilith had not been involved in the Fall. Her departure from Eden had been a free choice, not a punishment for disobedience, because at that time God had put no conditions on the perfected image of Herself. Her smile therefore was from before that aweful time: she had not felt the sadness of God as he walked in the Garden calling to his friends, and knowing as he called that they would never come again without fear. She had not heard him calling and she had not eaten the apple. Therefore her smile was free from both the knowledge of Evil and the sadness of it. Her smile was full of her own joy. At the back of her smile was the day of her creation and the knowledge of immortality; all the fruits of Eden were in that smile and so was the sight of First Water. Water that has not moved from its resting place, from the place of its own creation. That was in her smile and so was the sight of the animals who still knew their own true names, the Names by which they had been called out of chaos, before Man had given them his names and so mastered them. All these things were in her smile, but at the back of it. The first thing noticeable was her eagerness, the enthusiasm and optimism of her search and the proud knowledge that she could destroy, daily and without caring, as they were born, her hundred children and still be strong and free to search. But somewhere in her smile there was something else, something that Cain could almost recognise because he too had known exhaustion. Her smile was not beautiful like the smiles of women; it was without allure, it asked no questions and demanded no response. When Adam had awoken out of his sleep Eve had smiled at him, inviting him to make himself complete again, by taking her into him; invited him to give her existence, by coming into her, and it was Eve who taught women to smile. Cain knew that Lilith had not smiled for him but for herself alone, but even so he, who had spent so long avoiding all living creatures, was drawn to her. She had a smile that no one who has not met Lilith out in the Land of Nod, the strange land that is East of Eden, can imagine.

Cain had forgotten how to speak; he had been alone too long. When she greeted him by name, he tried to ask a question, but could not. She saw what he wanted to know and said, 'Do you know who I am?'

He shook his head.

'I am Lilith.'

He looked again, and she said,

'Then Adam never speaks of me? That is good. If he doesn't speak about me then he will soon stop thinking about me, and then he will forget me. That will be one less hold on me. I think that however he thought of me, I would be partly that, and I must be free of that too.

'Cain, it is difficult for me to say who Lilith is, for I am and am alone. To say not who, but what I am, is to speak of Lilith as she is to others, and I will be only for myself. But, but I will tell you this: God made Me and Adam in his own image. As he made hen and cock, ewe and ram, lioness and lion so he made Lilith and Adam in his own image, two and together one, male and female, husband and wife, together Man.'

Cain sat down watching her, always watching, hoping she would smile again, not knowing how to say the things he needed to say. She watched him, expecting him to question her claim, uninterested but waiting. Finally through nervousness and desire he found a monosyllable 'Eve?', and at the name of his mother he was filled with the memory of her, the warmth of her body and her arms around him. Her name spoken aloud, had a power that he had not known of, far stronger than any thoughts of her he had had. At the sound of her name she seemed to be present, seemed to be with him and he wanted to call her over and over again until she really was with him. As the sound faded away he knew absolutely, as he had never known before, that he was alone, that a man alone is a desolate being. He started to call her name again so as to feel her presence, but Lilith, stirred also by the name, though differently, began to speak again:

'Wife. She is a concubine, a slave, a whore. Worse, she is an invention of his own mind, Adam's mind. The day will come, not for a long time because she is clever and he is proud, and they will drug each other with lust and worship, but the day will come when he finds that his own idea of woman is not enough for his idea of himself as God; the day will come when he will grow brave and find that he does not want to be limited by his own mind. He will come out into the desert, come here to find the real female as God made her, the Free Being who does not know his mind as her source, who does not acknowledge him as her creator, and she whom he finds will be I. I am his wife in the Original Plan and he will not escape me for ever. But when he comes he will find that I am gone, that I do not need him. Then he will be alone.'

Cain tried another word; it was 'Mother?' and again, powerfully, he could see Eve, and his own wife with her arms round Enoch, their eldest child, he could see her sweat as she delivered him, and the smile as the baby sucked, and he saw that these things had been good and were a part of him from which he could not be separated. Lilith paused for a minute, the new swarm of children, self-begotten and hers alone, moved in her infinite womb; in the evening they would be born and she would suck them dry of their blood for her nourishment and would do so without a care. She felt no guilt because she was without knowledge of good and evil, and because she did not feel that this act had been imposed on her as a punishment, but as a bargain she had struck with God. No man could exist without other men and she was given the power to destroy in order to exist. But her offspring preparing for their birth did not know this and they moved within her in response to the distant thought of Cain and the word of 'Mother'. The movement could not move Lilith and she spat the word out.

'Mother. Mother. Eve has no self, and must seek an activity because she has no true Name. Every created thing but she has a true Name, a creation Name which is their place and power in the created firmness which rests upon the chaos. By their own Name they were called into form, out of void. Everything but she has heard their name as the Word moved on the face of the waters, and can answer to that Name when they are called again; when all is returned again to the Chaos they will answer to their Name and be saved. But she, she was not called, she was cut out of Adam. Her only Name is the one he gave her, 'woman', 'taken from man'. He named the animals too and because they did not know how to retaliate they accepted his names but they know they aren't true. Eve does not know her name and so she is his completely. But she feels the lack and looks for a Name. Only she does not dare go down into the darkness and void, where all Names are. She does not dare because that would take her too far from Adam and she fears that without him she will cease to exist; she might because she is not the daughter of Word and Chaos, but the daughter of Adam's dreams. She is afraid, as he dreamed her to be, because he had known me without fear and it was too much for him to bear. So she seeks for her Name in actions, in functions, relating always to him: mother, wife, companion, helpmeet.

'That is not the way. One day her daughters will realise that they cannot find their Name that way and they will come out to me. It will be hard for them. Every other created thing is created of God alone and partakes a little of his infinity. She was made by God, but not to his design. Her designer was limited by time and by desire. But in the end their need for a Name will be enormous and they will learn courage from that need and will come out into the desert and will live alone and will complete the search. But they will have to dare as I have dared; they will have to cast away knowledge of Other, and abandon Love, Obedience and Service, all the things by which Eve lives, by which she keeps herself alive. They will have to choose to hunt down themselves only, as I chose.'

Cain pushed the wild hair back from his forehead and wiped the pus off his hand on the rough grass. He was frightened, but now the idea of Wife and Mother had come back to him — even fear was better than being alone. He sought for another word, then echoed her saying, 'chose?'

'Of course I chose. I was in Eden. They could not send me. I was Free and I chose to be free. I flew out of Eden to the Red Sea. I flew.'

'How?'

'I named The Name.'

Cain screamed; and he heard it with delight, hoping it would blot out what she had said, but it faded in the bright desert air and Lilith said,

'I know it. Adam knew it too, but he preferred other knowledge. So long as we are involved in time and space we cannot contain everything and I must choose. I know the name, the true Name of the living God, and I dared to use that knowledge. I named the Ineffable Name and flew away from Eden. I despised the fat lands West of Eden, the Land of the Rivers; I despised the bright deserts where the tribes of your Father will wander. I flew to a place that is darker than desert, down in the Red Sea. They sent three angels after me, God sent his own angels after me, because he needed me, Lilith, for his plan, but I would not go back. Do you know why?'

But he did not dare to speak. For the first time he had learned the aweful power of words and he wanted to escape from what he had learned. She knew he did not dare and would have despised him if she had cared about Other, but she spoke for herself alone, and knew that he did not dare. Almost singing, chanting, rocking backwards and forwards, she went on:

'I was made with Adam — not from him, not after him, with him. We were created together and created equal. We were equal and he did not want to know it. He was afraid to know himself. Because we were the same, made in the image of God, because he did not know himself or God, see himself as God saw him, he would not touch me. We were both called from the Chaos together and saw each other being formed, saw each other more naked than naked; because he saw himself in me and was not strong enough to love himself, nor love the God that was nakedly in both of us, he would not touch me. He wanted me to make myself less so that he could love me without touching himself, touch me without knowing himself. Adam opened his eyes looking upwards and the first thing he saw was God, and he was frightened. But I saw myself first and was delighted. I am not going to make myself less in order to help another person escape from themselves. God can do that if he chooses, but not Lilith, not even for promises, like Love and Beauty and Service — and those were real words in Eden. I would not let Adam lessen me to lessen himself, and I was not afraid. I dared. I named The Name and flew away from Adam and from God. I dared. Even the chosen one, the awaited one will not dare. You will see. He will lessen himself for men, he will let them kill him, and the hour of his trial he will not use the Name. He will know the Name and know it to be his own, but he will not dare to use it. He will let them use their words for him, their own puny little words and names. He who is the Name, the Word and the Speaker will not dare. Only I have dared.'

She paused looking carefully out into the desert at something Cain could not see.

'Perhaps,' she said slowly, 'he will be right. He will have a long, long journey and no time for sleep. I have time, but he won't. Others and their need will hound him on; he will have to search out a new road as I have to, but he will have those desperate and frightened others. He will have to search in Lands lonelier than this one, and love will urge him on, harry and hunt him; that is why I have freed myself of those things. No, I will be tired for all eternity, that is the cost of courage. I have to sleep. I would not care except that sleep I have to take from him. My food I can make for myself, but I cannot make sleep.

'There was a bargain: I generate my own food, but I need his sleep, and need more and more because I used so much energy naming the Name. But I would pay that price, any price, to be free. But yet I need a little sleep.'

And Lilith fell asleep again, under the aloe tree and without moving. Her dreams and her thoughts came out of her; creeping from beneath her skin, breaking the surface and crawling, wriggling their way out into the desert: strange thoughts that Cain did not recognise although he watched carefully, and with fear. The thoughts, like real creatures, formed swellings under her skin and broke out: Lilith knew the Name and could create by word alone, almost, but she did not choose to give life, and only in her sleep could her thoughts free themselves. Cain did not understand, and after watching morbidly for a while he turned and watched her, still with fear. He had been alone for so long, and her very presence filled him with fear. She talked about things he did not dare think about, and cast doubt on the things he had been sure about and he was very frightened. But then, as she slept on and the shadows fell differently his loneliness came over him and with it a tenderness. He moved towards her; still huddled over himself, without changing his curious hunched position, he inched his way towards her.

She slept on. He watched. She slept. The sun crept across the sky and Cain was not alone.

He reached towards her, stretching his arm right out, far away from himself in a strange, pathetic gesture. Very gently Cain, the untouchable, touched Lilith. She moved in her sleep, but it was a comfortable movement. He placed a filthy hand on the side of her face and some of the tiredness seemed to go out of it. A thought seemed to rise in her mind, struggling towards the surface, hardly a thought, a new dream, but it failed to find a form for itself, for she too had been alone for a long time and she was very determined, but she did smile. Not the time that she had smiled before, but a half smile: a smile like Eve's smile in the evening when he and Abel, very young, very warm, had come in from the fields and the hills, and Adam had moved in his ancient unalienable gloom and maybe touched her gently on the side of the face, sadly but almost hopefully. The long nights of abstinence, caused by Adam's depression, his nightmares and his nerves were telling on both of them, and his sadness was eating into Eve. There was so little hope for either of them that even this half joke of Adam's would bring more of a smile to Eve's face.

As the sun was setting Lilith woke up. At first she seemed dazed, then realising that she was touched an enormous anger over-whelmed her, directed not at him but at herself. She struggled to rise, but her hundred children, now ready to be born held her down and her swinging hugeness hampered her. She was used to this and did not care; she needed the children to sustain her; she accepted them as part of the bargain she had driven with God. But she did gasp a little, for although, free from the curse of the Fall, she suffered no pain, there was effort. When she spoke, it was not to Cain, but to herself, 'I will not be touched. Not until the sun clothes me, the moon lies at my feet and the stars of heaven crown me. I will not. The search, the search.' Cain, frightened again but tempered by his tenderness, muttered after her, 'Search?' and she began again, 'Search. I am searching for myself. That is why I left Eden. That is why I am alone, why I destroy my children daily. I need them for food, I won't have them with me, needing me, deflecting me. They are nothing, everything is nothing. Somewhere is myself and I will find it. I will recreate myself beyond the limits of mind, the self I was before I was called out of Chaos by a name I did not choose myself. Yes I will go anywhere, even into the Water and Chaos if I can find a way. I can find a way. I will not be prevented, I will be free and have knowledge. Adam does not know how much he does not know. They fell because they accepted the limitations of their minds: Eve wanted to be like Adam, Adam like God; he would have known better if he had thought of me. I want to be Lilith — alone, unsupported, unaided, free. They fell through failure of imagina-tion, that's all, but I will not fail. Adam could not weaken me to be less, to give myself, to confuse myself with him, and with him to make others, and love them and bind myself with love. The angels who came to me in the Red Sea were beautiful too and loving; their love drew me to them, but I was strong, I did not want gifts, not even the gift of love and I would not go. I want to be myself, Lilith, Lilith, I, I, I. I would not become smaller, or give myself up. I came out into the Waste Places, where no one comes, and I am going to find Myself and learn that Self: the Self that is I, uncreated, untouched. I am going to seek myself and learn myself until I can call my own name and recreate myself, by myself, for myself, alone, as I generate my children. When I know my uncreated self, I will destroy this shape and send it back to Chaos and call myself out of Chaos again, alone. The search will be ended. I will go to God and he will take me, as Adam should have taken me, as Myself. He sent his angels to ask me to come back, but I will go freely when I have found myself beyond the limits of even his knowledge.'

Then she lay back and waited for her children to be born, spreading herself over the shadows. There was a richness and beauty in her ever fertile womb, and it heaved with life. The children were born beautiful and with the light of Eden in their eyes: they were born as her dreams had been, without pain, breaking the surface of her skin, between her thighs, and they lay smiling at the sinking sun. Lilith took each as it came. She set her long teeth into each neck and sucked the blood back into her body until there was nothing again and the desert was as barren as before, but she was stronger.

Cain wanted to speak. Years ago the words had come freely, speaking had been easy; but now there were no words and his tongue was heavy and slimy in his mouth. He did not understand. He thought of his wife writhing with delight in his arms and how he had been driven out into the Land of Nod, through his own fault, but in her arms had been Enoch, their promise of hope and relief. And he looked at Lilith and knew that her search was a long, long one, too long perhaps, but brave. He knew how long and how brave. And he thought again of Eve, and of the daughters that Enoch might have, and how they might have to come out here and be with Lilith and learn themselves and be alone, and he was sorry, but glad. And thinking of his wife and the long search, and because he had no words, he laughed.

Lilith turned to him; in her eyes he saw once more all the fruits of Eden, and he saw the hidden, guarded truth of male and female in the image of God, but he saw also that they were the same and together. They were very far away but they were not alone.

Then Lilith could bear no more company and she was gone.

Cain could not be alone any more. He left the Land of Nod and returned to the tents of his family. He did not dare to approach, so he haunted the woods, watching and loving. One day the blind king Lamech, son of Methusael, son of Mehujael, son of Irad, son of Enoch, son of Cain, went out hunting. His little son indicated something moving in the bushes and Lamech's arrow, for once, found its mark. It was Cain, who dies, smiling, in the bosom of his family.

An Edwardian Tableau

True to their word the Suffragists marched on the House of Commons yesterday, and the scenes witnessed exceeded in violence the utmost excesses of which even these militant women had previously been guilty.

It was an unending picture of shameful recklessness. Never before have otherwise sensible women gone so far in forgetting their womanhood.

Daily Sketch, Saturday, 19th November, 1910

DINNER SEEMED INTERMINABLE and yet Caroline was not sure that she wanted it to end. Afterwards there were two things to be faced; she was so tired that they seemed the same, equally important, equally unimportant, it did not seem to matter. Richard would propose to her and her mother would lecture her about coming down to dinner without stays. She knew the first from her father's heartiness; Richard and he had been in the library together before the other guests had arrived; also her mother at the last, the very last moment had changed the seating so that Caroline and Richard were sitting next to each other. And would she accept him? His face moved backwards and forwards, in and out of focus, she was so tired that she did not know what she would do, what she wanted. He would be a bishop one day they all said, he was a canon already, he was too old for her, she was too young for him, she would be a bishop's wife perhaps, perhaps not; How could she not know? How could she not care? She had known about the lecture from her mother at the very moment she had been walking down the stairs. How could she have thought that her mother, who noticed everything, would not notice? Her mother's standards, like her father's politics, were liberal but fixed, and Caroline knew every shade of them. She was allowed to smoke when there were no guests in the house; she was allowed to hunt escorted only by the groom if Graham was away, but not if he was at home and did not want to go out himself; and she could leave off stays in the daytime, but not in town and not for dinner. The lecture would cover these and other points and would include her mother's favourite little joke: 'Impropriety is one thing; indecency another.' She should not have risked it, she could not face it, the pain would have been better; no it wouldn't; even without the corset she could feel the pain, the bruise where only yesterday one of her whalebones had been snapped and driven up into her side. Hunting falls never hurt like this, but people were gentle over hunting falls and they were your own fault, or bad luck, not inflicted, deliberately laughingly inflicted, the way Graham had hurt her when they had both been very small — run to nurse and she would make it better — but now there was no nurse and no one she could tell. She was going to fall asleep, during dinner, at the table, no, please not, please not, God. They, the They out there, her mother, her father, stout Lady Corson, the They outside her pains and tiredness were talking — listen to them, don't fall asleep, not here, not here.

They were discussing some minor corruption, some political scandal. Something mildly bad, mildly important, Caroline could not remember the details. Sir George Corson kept saying how dreadful it was, how very dreadful, how it just went to show, how monstrous it was. Caroline's mother laughed her silvery laugh — and had her laugh always been like that or had she read somewhere of a silvery laugh and set out to procure one, just as she procured good cooks and beautiful dresses? — she laughed her beautiful, silvery laugh and said, 'Of course, Sir George, these things wouldn't happen if you gave women the Vote, now that would purify politics,' because of course Caroline's mother believed in the Vote in her beautiful decorous way. Sir George responded, true to form, 'Come now Mrs Allenby, women purify the Home, you make the politicians of the future and it's far too important a job for us to let you take time off to go running in and out of polling booths. You wouldn't like it if you have to do it, and you wouldn't be in a position to purify anything then you know. No, no, women don't need the Vote, they have the sons of England to look after, and they have husbands to do the sordid things like voting for them.' 'What about the unmarried women?' asked someone down the other end of the table; the conversation was going to become general, it always did when the Vote came up: there were subjects, the Vote, the Hysterical Militants, the Impossible Irish, the Ridiculous Workers, the Poor Peers, subjects that no one could resist. Sir George looked swiftly round the table, all the women were married except Caroline, who was very young, and anyway he could guess what was meant by the odd seating easily enough, so he laughed and said, 'The unmarried women? Dear Madam, there shouldn't be any, and in any case we don't want to be ruled by the failures, that's not democracy, not to my way of thinking. Remember a *Saturday Review* article that hit the nail on the head, said that a woman who failed to marry had failed in business and nothing can be done about that. I agree; may seem a little harsh at first, but think about it, think about it.' There was a little silence and then Richard raised his head and started speaking slowly, gently. Dear Richard, Caroline thought as his profile swam into focus, and yes they would make him a bishop and she would be a bishop's wife. 'It seems to me,' he was saying, 'that all this unrest is a symptom of a massive breakdown in trust. Everyone seems to be frightened, frightened and too proud. Women don't trust their men any more and the working people don't trust us. But it does seem to me that it must in some way be our fault, and if they can't trust us then we can't be worthy of the trust and must allow them something that they do trust, the Vote, or Unions, or Home Rule or whatever it is. I think they're wrong, I think they would do better to trust people than institutions, but they don't and they must somehow be freed from their fear. There's too much fear and not enough trust and love.'

Caroline's father laughed. 'Come now, Souesby, where there are separate interests there's going to be distrust. We don't trust the workers, come to that, and I for one don't trust the Irish, neither lot of them, and I don't trust those screaming women and I don't see my way to doing so. Universal love indeed; you sound like one of those Russian Anarchist fellows.'

But Richard was not daunted; he's brave, she thought, gentle but brave, just as he was out hunting. He went on, 'That's not fair, Sir, and you won't scare me from my truth with an anarchist bogey. I'm not an anarchist, as you know perfectly well, but I will say that I've read a fair bit of their literature and I think that in there somewhere there are some pretty sound ideas. Just building up more and more institutions is not going to help any of us; we must have more trust in each other, more common interest, and stop pinning our faith on all these organisations and machines, or at least look at them more closely and see if they deserve to continue.'

Someone said, 'That'a fine way for a good churchman to talk.'

He smiled and replied in his politest voice, 'Oh really, Sir, if you knew my record — a lunatic ritualist, practically an idolatrous papist, I assure you, you probably wouldn't think of me as a good churchman at all. I don't think I care so much about being a good churchman as I do about being a good man, and I still say that we all, all of us, on every side, need more love and more trust. Speaking as a churchman I could say simply that "Perfect love casteth out fear".' And even as she thought how superb he was, how her mother herself could scarcely have done it better, Caroline heard her own voice, in the distance, out there, say, 'So does hate.' And even then it might have been alright, but Richard, attentive and loving turned round and asked quite clearly what she had said and so there was no escape. For a timeless moment her eyes seemed fixed on her mother's beautiful chest, her pure white shoulders rising up from the exquisitely ruched chiffon and the line of her neck running up past her pearls and into her lovely, lovely hair, and why, thought Caroline into the endless gap in time, why don't I look like that so that I could say things like this and no one would mind? Then she said rather loudly, 'I said, "So does hate." Perfect hate casteth out fear.' And in the astonished silence that followed she could hear her head tapping out thoughts: That will teach them, that will teach them to sit here, so pompous and liberal and benign and intelligent and talk about purity and trust and love, when outside there is anger and meanness and hate, beautiful hate which made you feel six foot tall, which made you feel as you felt when you knew that your mare was going to take in her stride a fence that others were refusing at. That will teach you Canon Richard Souesby to keep your white hands clean and turn the other cheek and trust them all while they beat you and throw you about and laugh in your face. And then Lady Corson, kind, well-meaning, fat Lady Corson said loudly and carefully, 'That reminds me of the most peculiar book I was reading, young women are so much more imaginative I think than we ever were. I wonder if you've heard of it, Mr Allenby? It's called *Dreams* by a Miss Olive Schreiner, a colonial I believe. It was lent to me by...' And they went on talking and gradually everyone joined in, but not Richard; he sat beside her, did not look at her, looked at his food, and Caroline was afraid, afraid for herself, afraid of herself, and now he would not marry her and what would she do? How would she manage without him? How could she have thought that she did not care, that it did not matter? And now he would never ask her and she loved him, she loved him, she loved him. But he did not turn round, did not smile, just sat looking at his food and eating it. And her mother's chilly white shoulders were waiting, waiting till afterwards, till all the people had gone and the fact that she was not wearing stays had ceased to matter compared to what she had done, she had silenced a whole dinner party, she had embarrassed people. The cold white shoulders and the tiredness and the dreadful, dreadful pain in her side all became one cold blur and Richard would not ask her to marry him and she was getting colder and colder and further and further away and then Emma was beside her and 'would Miss Caroline like a glass of water?' Dear Emma, quietly pouring water and she drinking it quietly and feeling better and the room coming back towards her and she back into it, all so quietly that no one noticed. No one except Richard and he turned towards her looking concerned and asked almost soundlessly if she was alright. He smiled sweetly lovingly, and she thought that after all he would ask her to marry him and she would accept and he would look after her always, and she felt well and strong again and started listening to the conversation.

By now it had moved on to the Awful Incident the day before, when hundreds of women had fought with the police for six hours trying to get into the House of Commons. Well, she thought, it was bound to come up, it was just bound to. She felt strong enough for it, she need not say anything, they need never know, she need only listen, even the pain seemed bearable. Sir George was talking again, 'I don't often find myself agreeing with that dreadful *Mirror*. This time I did, they hit the nail on head, *The Times* was far too soft on them. *The Mirror* said those women were a disgrace to the Empire and a source of shame to all womanhood. Couldn't agree more. Glad they left the word "ladies" out. I wouldn't even call them "women"; females that's what they are, females. Disgusting.' And no she couldn't keep quiet, could not listen and say nothing, could not hear her friends spoken of like that, because they were her friends, so she said, 'I was there.' She saw the rucheing of her mother's dress move as her shoulders tightened invisibly disapproving. Then one of the ladies down the table said, 'Caroline dear, I didn't know you were a militant,' and there was perhaps a hint, a slight tone of admiration, envy. It was not clear, but it was enough for Caroline to go on. 'Oh, no, I wasn't. I mean I'm not a member of the Union or anything. I was there by mistake, but I got involved, because of the crowd and separated from Emma, there was this enormous crowd, watching them you know.' How could she be so cool? Her mother's shoulders had relaxed again, she could go on, there would be no trouble, so long as she kept calm. 'I didn't understand the newspapers this morning, it didn't seem like that then, there, the police were very brutal.' Sir George interrupted, 'Now, now Miss Allenby, they were only doing their duty.' 'I thought,' she said, as carefully as possible, 'that it was their duty to arrest anyone who assaulted them. They wouldn't arrest us.' The shoulders tightened again. Was her whole life to be governed by the rise and fall of a pair of perfect, beautiful shoulders? 'You see,' she hurried on, 'I got involved.' Involved. There must be a better word: committed, converted. She had been standing, pushed about by the crowd, trying to see Emma, when suddenly a funny old — no not old, middle-aged — lady had fallen to the ground at her feet. She had bent down to help and asked, 'Are you all right?' But the woman was hysterical, she lay on the ground and sobbed, 'They won't arrest us, they won't arrest us, they won't arrest us' over and over again. How could she explain to these safe people how nothing had made sense, how the police were refusing to arrest them; them, us, me? 'Sir George, you don't understand, the crowd was all round, pushing in; if one tried to get out, and at first I tried very hard, I did not want to be there, I don't believe that militancy will work, I didn't see the point of it, I wanted to get out, but if you tried to leave then horrible men in the crowd pushed you back in again, back to the police and they would not arrest you whatever you did. There was an old lady there in a wheel chair, perhaps she was as mad as anything, perhaps she should have stayed at home, but she was there, and the police pulled her out of her chair and threw her to the ground and then they shoved the chair away; I saw them do that. It was very frightening, if the ladies did foolish things it was because they were frightened.' The panic had been the worst thing, she had been so frightened, so lost, so confused, turning in circles, pushing against other women, pushing them down, knocking them over herself in her desperate efforts to escape. Finally she had run into a policeman and had grabbed him thinking that here was safety, that he would help her, 'Get me out of here, please get me out of here.' He had seized her in his arms, crushing her so tightly that she could hardly breathe, tearing her blouse on his buttons, and he had tried to kiss her, his thick mouth on hers, and when she had protested wordlessly, determinedly, he had laughed and said, 'That's what you really want, that's what you're here for, isn't it?' She had started to struggle, kick, even bite. The policeman suddenly angry, no longer smiling had literally thrown her onto the ground and as she landed she had felt one of her stays snap and ram itself up between her ribs. The pain and the shock had been outrageous and she had lain there with a red film running over her eyes for a moment, and then she had opened her eyes and seen the policeman standing there smiling, pointing her out to another of himself who was also smiling, but who looked almost frightened. A great wave of hatred, the sort she had not felt since she had been a little girl, filled her up, lifted her to her feet and she had realised that she was not frightened any more. She was a fighting force, she was Deborah and Joan of Arc, and Boadicea and there was no fear but only waves of beautiful hatred which make her feel six foot tall and insuperable. Hitting and shoving and insulting policemen had felt like Mafeking Night, only the bonfires were all inside her and hotter and brighter and better. But these things she could not explain, and she said, still quite calmly, to the dinner party, 'You cannot imagine how horrible it was, how frightening; some of the Members of Parliament came out on the steps to watch, they were smiling and laughing. One of them had a little child with him, she cannot have been more than ten, and he kept pointing us out to her and trying to make her laugh and she just stood there and looked amazed. He is probably a good honest man who would not go himself, let alone take his daughter to a fight, a match, whatever it is that men go to, Father, what's the word? I know, a "mill", but he still thought that seeing a thousand women abused by the police, English ladies by their own police, was a suitable amusement for her. And all those women were doing was trying to present a petition, asking for what they believe to be their rights. Apart from the Vote, surely they have a right to petition Parliament? I hated that Member of Parliament so much at that moment that even if they had been fighting for something that I thought bad, totally wrong, I would not have left those women then, I would not have wanted to, even if I'd been able.' She was getting excited, she knew it was a mistake, that it might spoil everything, that it would do the suffrage cause no good; but her excitement was not for the Cause, it was for herself, because she had discovered that she did not need to be afraid, that she could be strong, that she need not be tied down in awe of her mother, that beauty was unimportant compared to the strength of her feelings, that militancy might not do much good for its cause but it did wonderful things for the militants. They knew what she knew, how good it was to be angry, to be really angry and show it, that when you were really angry nothing else mattered, that there was no pain, no fear, no restraint, no anything but an enormous space you could fill up with yourself and see how huge and strong you really were. She knew now how good it was to have an enemy and know that he hated and feared you, because the police had been frightened of the women and of what they had found in themselves, but that you only hated and were not frightened so that you could win really even when they appeared to have won. And so she finished up, almost panting, 'Sir George, I have told you how dreadful it was, how humiliating and disgusting, how shameful to the Government that let it happen. I haven't told you, I cannot tell you, how fine it was, how good I felt fighting and hating the police, how good it was to abuse Members of Parliament at the top of my voice, how fine and beautiful and lovely those muddy women on the ground were, how much I loved those "Females" as you call them when we helped each other. They have been waiting, all women, We have been waiting for fifty years for the Vote, waiting patiently to accept it as a pretty present from the men who laugh at us, who abuse us mentally and physically. I can tell you, after yesterday I am beginning to believe that after thirty years of patience and waiting and teaching calmly, Our Lord must really have enjoyed hurling over the tables of the money lenders in the temple.'

'Caroline! That is quite enough!' That was her Father, his good-natured face red with embarrassment. Her mother, of course, was calmer and far colder; 'Well, I think we've heard quite enough about the hysterical conduct of some unhappy and unbalanced women for one evening. Emma, some more fruit shape for Mrs Lettering please. Tell me Sir George, have you seen the Martins since they got back from Dresden? One can't help wondering why they've returned just now.'

Caroline sat at her place and the warmth she had felt died away, but she wasn't sorry, she could not be sorry, neither for what she'd done nor for what she had said. She would be sorry in the morning when she had to listen to her mother and watch the beautiful neck take on its curve of disdain; she would be sorry if Richard did not ask her to marry him and sorrier still when he married someone else, but it would not be the right kind of sorry, not the kind they would expect. That kind was out of the question now she knew how strong she could be, how it felt to be free of fear, how it felt to be totally herself. Then she looked at Richard and he was smiling, not pityingly, not even kindly, but with open admiration, even respect. For a moment she was tempted towards humility, towards wondering what she had done to deserve this wonderful man, but her courage was high and with a final triumphant rush of bravery she thought, 'Of course I have deserved it, of course I deserve this man, of course.'

Andromeda

MY MOTHER WOULD say that it was wrong to call one's husband a thief. Mine is. Thief, thief, thief, I scream at him silently.

My mother would say that it was worse than wrong to hate one's husband, to stay awake through the night and pray for his death. I do. Die, die. I curse him while he sleeps.

My mother would say that it was the worst crime to loathe one's children and wish they had never been born. I do that too.

My mother was a great queen, a beautiful woman and a loving mother. She fed me at her own royal breast until I was more than five years old. I can remember the sweet whiteness and warmth of her cradling me. Like a queen bee in a hive I was fed on royal jelly. I slept in her bed with her until I was nearly grown up. If I woke in the night she would stroke me and soothe me back into gentle dreams, holding me close against her own softness.

My father was a king, a true hero; he sailed with the Argonauts on the last great adventure of the golden age. I hardly knew him, but I knew his devotion to my mother and to me.

My husband is a thief, a bastard and a patricide.

Perseus the Golden, son of Zeus, slayer of the Gorgon, saviour of Andromeda, founder of Mycenae. Ha.

They don't know I'm mad. No one knows I'm mad. It's my own secret. I guard it closer than I guard my life. It's mine, the only thing of my own that he has left me. I will die before I let him take that too. My madness and my hatred: fed on the milk I would not feed my children, nursed on the breast where I would not nurse my sons.

Perseus' queen walks gently through his palace, a model wife, calm but busy, her eyes lowered, veiled by her long dark lashes, an example to all young women in her modesty, her humility, the love and duty that she bears towards her husband; she seldom raises her eyes except to smile benignly at her husband's subjects or sweetly, gratefully at him.

But Andromeda is mad, mad, mad, and no one knows. In the night she roams the palace, nursing the famous dagger with which her husband killed the Gorgon, planning her thrusts, in and out, in and out; blows of vengeance that would make her more famous even than he. He claims that Pallas Athena gave him her helmet to make him invisible. I need no helmet: no one is more invisible than his own good, gentle, devoted wife. That is more than helmet, it is a whole armour of invisibility, which the mad woman wears all day and is safe. Mercifully he is also a fool. There are days when I sit beside him at the table eating my meal and watching him through my meek, humble eyes, watching him shovel his food between his thick red lips, watching his coarse mouth masticate and his throat heave as he swallows it down, and wishing each mouthful was snakes' venom. And I think, How can he be so stupid? How can he fail to feel the waves of poison pour out of me and into his food, thrusting down and into his innards, as he has thrust his poison into mine? And then he will turn to me and say in his silly, sickly, smiling voice, 'My Andromeda, aren't you hungry? Don't you like this food? You eat like a bird, my little chicken.' And he may pick up some revolting morsel and try to feed me with his own sweaty, blood-stained hands.

When I was a child I sat on the laps of my mother's eunuchs and they would feed me sweets and peaches, their soft rounded fingers caressing my hair, and I would hop like a humming bird from silky nest to silky nest, or come to rest against my mother's naked arm and she would reach for a grape for me; or I would bury my face in her warm sweet-smelling stomach and taste the softness of her for a dark moment.

He bangs and crashes, leaping up from the table, calling for more wine, shouting at his friends, bantering crudely, challenging someone to some absurd contest, stripping off his tunic, yelling for his horse, his slaves, his hounds, his spear. Pausing only to stroke the gold hair on his chest with a little tender gesture, he dashes outside and for hours I have to hear the wild shouts and confused arguing from the gymnasium or the arena. Then he comes puffing in again, victorious, sweaty, performing, crying out, 'Admire Me, Admire Me.' It is not an appeal, it is an expression of his conviction that I and everyone else in the world must share his admiration of himself. He believes that I admire him, because he totally believes that he is admirable. He notices nothing; not even the fact that his subjects and so-called friends always let him win every game, being sensible men and as aware as I am which way survival lies. Certainly he does not notice that the golden hairs he strokes are fading and yellowish, or that the famous manly chest is slipping lower. Oh yes, he's a fool my husband, as well as a thief.

But sometimes I do envy him his perfect, unshakeable arrogance and blindness. He can see everything exactly as he wants it to be. His loving wife. His fine sons, his chaste daughter. His enthusiastic subjects. And above all his heroic wonderful self. I tell you seriously, he sincerely believes that he is actually, literally the son of Zeus. His mother's family were very strict and she was kept permanently under guard to keep her chaste. It didn't work, she became pregnant from 'a shower of gold' as popular idiom has it: the only thing that anyone knows about my husband's father is that he was rich enough to bribe the guards. But Perseus has chosen from childhood to take it literally. His mother was imprisoned, but beloved of the Gods; and Zeus disguised himself as a shower of gold in order to impregnate her. We got on rather well his mother and I. We shared something in common; we had both been driven mad by him — she through devotion and I through hatred — mad to the point that we could see through him. We never spoke of it, but just occasionally we would exchange tiny glances of amusement, of complicity from beneath our chastely lowered lashes.

Sometimes I really cannot believe that a grown man can accept these self-created delusions as historical facts, but if you start from an unassailable assumption that you are perfect anything and everything becomes perfectly logical. Even killing his grandfather was his destiny under heaven and NOT His Fault: nothing at all to do with his showing off and lethal competitiveness. Of course the great advantage of being a king is that you can deal very effectively with anyone foolish enough to express a contrary opinion. Which is one of the reasons why I keep quiet. I am going to live to see him dead. With my own wifely hands I shall perform my ritual office. I am disgusted I say publicly, by those queens who employ professional substitutes. 'How brave, how devoted, how good our queen is,' they murmur. With my own hands I am going to wipe that smug smile off his face; gently and with such joy I am going to close those pretty blue eyes; and then, when he is no longer watching me, I shall spit in his face and laugh. I shall wear the full heavy royal mourning veil when we process to his mausoleum. I shall wear it so that no one shall see the unholy glee on my face when they seal up that body for the worms to devour.

Yes, yes, I long to see you then, Perseus the Golden, the favourite
of the Gods, with the worms boring and thrusting down into your
bloated flesh and growing fat on your decay. They are on my side,
King of Mycenae. Everything you have stolen from me they will
steal back again, strip away the layers of beauty and complacency,
and expose what I have known from the very beginning — the
stinking, putrifying foulness of your inner being, my dear husband, my own sweet royal lord. You thief, you fat arrogant hog of
a petty thief. They hang men like you daily in the courtyard and I
lean out of the window, secretly, and imagine it is you, rotting,
with the birds picking out your eyes. I laugh and laugh, heroic
slayer of the Gorgon, to think how little those snaky tresses will
help you then.

When I was a child they called me their little bird, as I pecked
and chirped and sang through that sunny palace. I long and desire
to chirp as I peck at your dead eyes, and to sing as the worms
destroy your proud manhood.

His pride is at the root of him. He is that and nothing more. It is
easy to understand. Yes, I can be understanding too, I can say how
hard it must be to be a landless child, a fatherless son at the mercy
of a whim of charity from foreigners, cast away unwanted and
unrecognised by his own family. I can understand what that lack
would do to a pretty, able child and to a passionate headstrong
adolescent. I can understand how the lust to say 'Mine', to own, to
possess, to lay claim to everything, would grow in a person from
that background. Understand, yes. Forgive, tolerate, even care?
No. No, because it is not right; but No even more because I am
one of the things possessed, taken over, made into his. His, His,
Everything has to be His. 'It was love at first sight,' he says of me.
'As soon as I saw her I knew that I would run any risk, dare any
adventure, if I could make her my own. Don't believe anyone who
says there is no such thing as love at first sight. We knew better,
don't we, my own?'

Love at first sight. It was jealousy at first sight. He was passing
through Ethiopia and found that someone else was the hero of the
moment. That was the intolerable thing: that someone else, not
him, had laid claim to a moment of history. He could not endure
that. If love was the price of grabbing one more occasion to be the
Great Hero he was more than willing to pay it. But for me it was
my moment. The moment that I chose, that I had dedicated to
myself, my one chance, the one time when I had a choice and
could offer myself as something more than the little princess,

their bird, their darling. I was to be the pure, the chosen symbol of my mother's love for her people. The only acceptable sacrifice, the only freely offered gift. Can you understand? When the sea monster raged up from the deep my happy homeland was turned overnight into a place of despair. And only I could save them. I offered myself as a sacrifice for my city. The perfect sacrifice has to be offered voluntarily. I offered. What were my motives? Love, I say; my one true impulse of love. Perhaps there were other things in it too; things that were less pure, dark poisoned things. But it was my decision for my life; my own moment of choice and I chose it. The mixture of joy and grief that greeted my offer confirmed me. They all needed me in a way that is very rarely offered to women.

How can I describe it? There was an hysteria in me and in the whole city for the week of the ritual purification. Was it here that the seeds of my madness were sown? I know that is possible, but if things had fallen out as they were meant to, what would my madness or sanity have mattered?

The rituals are complex and, to the uninitiate, uninteresting — the important fact is the growing separateness of the chosen victim. I had to move from the palace to a special, appointed room inside the temple. The day before the last day my mother came to say goodbye to me, she was the last person allowed to do so. I had not seen my father since the second day. After this farewell she would not be allowed to touch me or even speak to me. I lay in her arms, neither of us weeping, just tender and close. She petted me, kissed and embraced me. Her last words to me were, 'My sweet heart, I'm heartbroken, but for myself, not for you. I almost envy you. I'm glad. I love you so much, I could never have borne losing you. I always wanted to do this, to be able to keep you pure and safe and free from so much. And now you'll never have to know. O treasure, sweet heart. A bride of the sea, the sweet clean gentle sea. Oh my beloved, be strong.' For the last time I buried myself in her softness, the two of us twined together, our lips against each other's. But when she went I felt only a growing excitement and uncertainty.

In the morning the priestesses came to dress me. The soft white dress felt like my mother's last caress, but the scent of the flowers was almost overwhelming, sweet and cloying; a heady contrast to the rich bitter smell of the incense. My head began to swim and my stomach contract in nervous, thrilling spasms. The hands of the priestesses seemed to dance over my body and my skin sang out for more. I wanted to rush into the sea, now, to have it around me, embracing me, entering and consuming me. We set off in slow procession for the half mile to the shore. The jewel green sheep-cropped sea grass seemed as buoyant as waves and the sea daisies too blindingly white. The sun warmed the back of my neck as it rose over the city and through the thin white robe I could feel the breeze with every corner of my skin. Where the grass comes to an end and the firm sand beach begins we stopped. About fifty yards away, where the water begins, there is a jagged outcrop of rocks on the seaward side on which I would wait, invisible from the land, totally exposed to the sea. A priestess bent down and cut my sandal thongs so that I could step out of them. I raised my arms and cried my intention to the sea, that I came freely to be given to the sea, by my people, in love and duty. Then the priestess cut the bands that held my hair, and the back of my neck was suddenly cool where it was protected from the sun. Again I called out that without ties and freely I offered myself to the sea. Then finally the priestess cut through the girdle and shoulder of my dress and it fell gently down my body. I stepped out of the pool of cloth at my feet and naked began to walk along the marked out path to the rock. Golden sand, white naked flesh, and the solemn Lament of the Maiden began. To its beautiful notes I walked round the rock and out of life.

The waves lapped my feet, cold despite the sun, and the sea was very bright. I remember quite clearly hearing the sound of the lament, feeling the cool dampness of the rock behind me and revelling in a moment of joy and fierce expectation. Then the sun seemed to quiver . . . a moment of unnatural stillness . . . four huge waves lashed out at me . . . beating me down . . . onto the rock. The hot strong waves of the monster's breath. I wanted them . . . fought to receive the full impact of them . . . embracing their thrust . . . feeling them soak deep into me.

I caught a glance,
      hardly that,   a physical sensation
    golden.   The lion that hunts
with his mane as the waves.
I don't know,
don't remember,
can't describe.
I leaned, longingly, lovingly, towards that hot mouth . . . to finish all things with its welcome.

And sweaty and muscle bound He ripped me from my triumph.

With the help of that serpented profanity of his he stole my moment and made it his. I didn't know at once what had happened, but I did know, heart-breakingly, that something had gone absolutely and forever wrong. He could not allow anyone else so much as a single instant of courage or generosity. He stole it. He stole my moment, robbed me of my own choice, violated my sacrifice. He stole the one thing I had; stole it, possessed it and made it his own.

What else he and his snake friend stole from me I do not like to think of.

Well, in the eyes of the world I have been a good wife to him. I never saw that I had any choice: He stole my moment from me and I was never granted another. But my husband is a thief and in those depths of me that even he can never ravage, I revile him.

The Tale of the Beautiful Princess Kalito

ONCE UPON A time, long, long ago and far, far away — if that makes it any easier — there lived The Beautiful Princess Kalito.

The Beautiful Princess Kalito really was very beautiful: she had skin the colour of pure strained honey waiting warm and soft in the sunshine — golden with hints of darkness, but smooth and cool and glowing like the skin of a ripe cherry. She had soft black eyes, painted smoothly onto her cheeks with a disciplined, apparently casual brush stroke and her mouth was little and round and pink. Her fringe of hair lay on her forehead like mulberry silk, dyed black with all the skills of the northern dyers. She had a little round soft body. She had very tiny feet and no name. None of this is surprising.

She had always been beautiful, even as a little child; moreover she had then had feet which, while pretty of course, had been of a perfectly ordinary and uninteresting size, suitable in every way for a pretty, active and rich little princess. She had also had a name then, although she was now not always able to remember what it had been. She had abandoned it on marriage. The Beautiful Princess Kalito, understandably, was not her name, but a title indicating that she was her husband's wife.

The Beautiful Princess Kalito, as well as having a very important and highly placed husband, had also had an extensive palace: at least she understood that it was extensive, because an extensive palace is one of the things that The Beautiful Princess Kalito had every right to expect, along with not having a name and having very tiny feet. She had not of course seen much of it, but what she had seen was, like herself, precious and beautiful. There were gardens of intricate delicacy, where water-wheels turned musically and lotus flowers — blood red and milk white — flowered immaculate, and water lilies floated serenely on ponds deep with golden fish. And the gardens changed magically, gently, into pagodas and terraces of wrought wood, where birds in cages sang tunes of entrancing loveliness. And the terraces, too, dissolved through trellises and archways into rooms where more lotus flowers — redder than blood and whiter than milk — flowered on the walls with an even finer perfection than those in the gardens; where golden fishes swam forever across walls of water-lilies; where at every turn huntsmen on horses, with long spears and dogs, chased deer of slenderness and grace around pagodas more intricate and refined than those in the garden — and did so without the noise and the sweat and the disturbance that her husband complained of on those few occasions when he could bring himself to leave those disagreeable pursuits and spend an evening of perfect joy, 'in heaven, beloved, in heaven' with her.

The Beautiful Princess Kalito also had three sons, who had once been golden tumbling bundles of delight with little thatched lids of black hair, and shiny black eyes who had played and giggled around her feet when their nurses brought them in to her. They had once climbed on to her lap and stood with their arms round her neck and gazed levelly into her eyes with glorious smiles of pure devotion, but who now had gone away and when they appeared at all it was to look at her with nervous scorn through hard black lenses. The Beautiful Princess Kalito did not have any daughters; but she did have piles of silk cushions which exuded a warm rich smell, and cases of jewels which glowed and stabbed at the darkness when her maid-servant opened the caskets and selected the appropriate items for The Beautiful Princess Kalito to wear. And she had porcelain bowls so fine that the light filtered through them in colours strange and rich — blues and crimson and flame. And she had horses of bronze and clay which stood with a military stiffness and an interesting greenish tinge. And she had jade palaquins carved far away and so fragile in their perfection that breath could shatter them. And she had gold ornaments so fine as to need no purpose, or use, or explanation. And she had a carved wall of pink stone and white stone with plants growing from it here and there, which kept her and all her husband's other treasures safe from all eyes. What more could any beautiful princess wish for?

The Beautiful Princess Kalito had, moreover, memories. She could remember when her sons were a delight and a refuge for her. She could remember before that, when her servants looked at her with admiration and envy. She could remember when her husband spent time with her in joy. On golden sunlit evenings when the blossom of her trees cast a special light in the garden, she could even remember how it was when she could run and dance and live without pain. And in the late watches of the night, when the huge fierce stars gaped coldly at her, she could, just sometimes remember the day when all simplicity of joy had ended.

Although The Beautiful Princess Kalito had little to do all day and nothing to do most nights, three times a week, at the very least, she had an important and private engagement. Then they would bring to her very inner and most private room great bowls of warm scented water and herbs and unguents and oils, all strongly redolent and heady in their sweetness like overblown hyacinths. The richness of their savour would creep up her little curved nostrils and weave about in her brain until she nearly fainted with the excess of their beauty. And there, alone and unattended, The Beautiful Princess Kalito would ceremoniously take off her clean-every-morning knitted white cotton over-socks and start to unwrap and clean her feet. As she ritually unbound the bandages a new smell would start to contend with the giddy scents of her room. They were at war with each other: the perfumes of the master perfumers of the Great Empire and the stink of the rotting, unaired, dead flesh of The Beautiful Princess Kalito's tiny feet.

When the last bandage was off and the nakedness of her feet exposed, the stench from them would overwhelm the room. Then taking the dead flesh in her hands, The Beautiful Princess Kalito would lower the inanimate hunks into the warm scented water. She would prize the hooked claw of the big toe with its soft spongy nail away from the petal-like mass of where her other toes had once been and scoop out the new white dead matter from the space. She would tenderly scrape the freshly putrefied gunge from around her heels and pry into the crevasses of the rounded slug which made up the middle part of that glob. Each object was only four inches long and still it would take her over an hour to wash and re-perfume them. Then, finally satisfied, taking up the new pile of white bandages, the new pots of sweet scented oils and creams, she would re-bandage them. There was a point at the centre of this process when she would be tempted to despair; when it seemed impossible that even the softest bleached wool, even the incense of the whole world, would be able to cover over that stink of putrefaction. But always, by the end, she would have won, would have ordered all things aright, and pulling on the delicately knitted over-socks, she would toddle back into her world; her feet, the lotus flowers of her husband's heart, restored, perfect.

Her husband too, incidentally, had fine feet; long and straight with a high delicate arch. Each toe, to her early amusement and delighted fascination, was separated and could be flexed individually. When she was first married she had very much wanted to touch them as he did hers. 'Ah, my love,' he would say, 'Ah, my beautiful princess.' He would hold those tiny, tender, white as mountain snows little socks, each in the palm of his hand, squeezing them, caressing them; leaning over her, folding her soft little body almost in half, he would place each immaculate little cotton bundle against the soft golden skin above his brown nipples, just where the secret hiddenness of his underarm met the bold openness of his chest and seem almost to swoon with joy. Recovering physically, he would press down on her, now almost out of his mind with passion, so that the weight on her never-exercised muscles hurt — but what was the hurt compared with the pleasure that she could give him, the amount that he loved her? 'Ah, my lotus flower, ah, pearl of all my riches, ah, see these perfect . . .' he could scarcely even speak for his entrancement, 'For me, for me. Oh I will love you always and always, because my precious can never run away. See each little mouse, hiding in its scented hole, that is what my beautiful little princess is for me. See these feet, so tiny, so perfect, that my love could dance on a lotus flower and not bend or crush one petal of it.' But as, in fact, The Beautiful Princess Kalito could not dance at all, he would have to call in dancing girls to inspire his erotic imagination further and they would lie together watching the dancing girls disrobe, while she tried neither to giggle nor to weep and he fondled and turned and twisted and hurt The Beautiful Princess Kalito's beautiful little lotus-flower feet.

And after all it was precisely for this that her mother, weeping, had called her in from her games with her brothers one day when she was seven years old. Weeping, laughing, she had told her daughter that she was now old enough to become a woman. Tickling, teasing, she had wrapped the first soft bandages, sung the first binding songs, trying through her tears to tell her daughter the old stories. How the Emperor had bound the feet of his favourite dancing girl, long, long ago and far, far away, so that she could dance for him on a lotus flower and not bend nor crush one petal of it. How, despite the pain, one day, when her little daughter lay so soft and sweet with her tiny feet against the chest of her lover and her lord, just where the secret hiddenness of his armpit met the bold openness of his chest, she would sing and praise the tiny feet which bound her lover to her with a tighter binding than any which might now seem to hurt her. And together they laughed and the bandages were made tighter and tighter. But The Beautiful Princess Kalito — although then of course she was no such thing, but a pretty little girl who played in the rich acres of her noble father's cherry trees — The Beautiful Princess Kalito was allowed to sit with her mother and her aunts and her grand-mother all day and be counted by them as a grown-up, as a woman. So that it was not until some days later that she dis-covered that she could no longer run down to the stream and dabble her toes in its icy coldness until each individually they wriggled up, rearing away from the water until she laughed and had pity on them.

That night when the little girl was unable to settle down to sleep because of the unaccustomed tightness — too extreme yet to call it pain, although there would be nights and nights to come when pain would be a gentle and kindly word for what that child was to endure — she was surprised to hear her mother sobbing and sobbing in the next room. Her mother, who was a great lady and the wife of a great warrior prince, sobbing so loudly, so inelegant-ly. Then she heard her aunt come toddling in on her tiny feet and sit beside her sister and mutter sweetly, softly as women do with each other when there is great grief and nothing to be done about it. The child heard one remark only with any clarity; the aunt said to the mother, 'Sweet, you know what they say, if we love our daughters we cannot love their feet.' A pause, and then moving from the old proverb to her own sharp merry tone, the aunt laughed loudly, though not very happily, and said, 'We love the daughters, the men love their feet . . . it all works out I suppose.'

And indeed her aunt was right, because her husband did love her feet. As described earlier and so on and so on. She loved his feet too, as it happened, but once she had tried to take them in her hands — or rather to take one of them, for her sweet little hands could not encompass even one of his fine-boned feet. At the time, which was quite soon after they were married, he was lying back in that joyful exhaustion she could never understand. The silk cushions were piled around him and he was beautiful and he loved her and he had given her a palace and he spent every evening with her. She was filled with a new and restless feeling which she did not recognise, growing perhaps from somewhere near the base of her smooth golden belly. She sat up giggling with her legs crossed under her, and she did of course look sweet and enchanting and very young and innocent, as well as beautiful. She picked up one of his feet and, bending forward, inserted her little tongue into the space between his largest toe and the one next to it. They had a strong flavour of salt and a smell of grass and goats. She turned the foot back at the ankle and her tongue went exploring the stiff firm arc of his instep, while her fingers felt the powerful tension in his tendon, running up from heel to leg and then, perhaps, on upwards. He lay back sighing and she let her mouth wander on in the enchanted valleys and the mountain ranges and the forests of his foot. And the restless feeling ran up from the base of her stomach to her tongue and back again like a silk cord that tightened and tightened and also somehow spread outwards so that her fingers and her back too were caught in the cord, were part of the cord, and she toppled forward and lay out beside him, her fine silk shift rumpled up on her soft honey coloured thighs which were unable any longer to remain still, and she sucked and groped at his feet and knew that something was going to happen.

And something did. He changed from liquid delight into iron. He sat up. He said, 'That's quite enough.' He pulled his foot away. He got up and left the room, his back expressing displeasure.

And after that, although she never repeated the experiment; although she never asked, not even herself, what the purpose and meaning of that strange tight cord might be; although his sons grew in her body and were born with little round bodies and flabby squashed feet just like hers; although they grew up with straight fine bodies and tough strong feet just like his; although she was beautiful and sat in her beautiful palace; although she allowed him, whenever he wanted, to take her little lotus-flower cotton socks in his hands and croon to them; although she was as good as the gold she both resembled and was adorned with — still he came less and less often to her part of the extensive palace and from the pitying looks and half heard gossip of her servants she knew that he was keeping concubines — neither as well born nor as beautiful as she, but able to please him without challenge, without questions.

So there she was, The Beautiful Princess Kalito, and time went by. And what with dressing up in the morning and again in the evening, and washing her feet three times a week, and wondering if her husband would come and visit her in the evenings, she probably had as much to do as was good for any beautiful princess in a story.

But one day something new happened. She was toddling around the extensive palace and quite by chance she found a new room. It was a pretty little room, high up in the palace and hung with the most exquisite silk paintings. It had obviously been the favourite room of some other Beautiful Princess Kalito before her and the idea of this tenuous link appealed to her somehow and she took to sitting there sometimes on her silken cushions to sip her tea. And after another little while she discovered that her pretty little room had a little window and that the windows looked out over the filigree wall of pink and white stone and into an orchard of fruit trees very like the one she had played in with her brothers many, many years before. And she grew to like to look out of the window at the orchard, and with a caution quite unbecoming to a beautiful princess, she never mentioned to her husband that she sometimes sat in this little room, and sometimes looked out of the window. But then, he really did not come very often, and when he did they really had far more important things to be doing and thinking of than in which of her many rooms the princess liked to sit and drink her tea.

So, gradually, as she heard that her sons had married in their turns beautiful princesses with soft painted eyes, tiny feet and no names either; and as she met these younger women and was forced to know that she was no longer quite as beautiful as she had been; and as she discovered again the joy of plump babies in her grandsons and discovered again that they grew up and vanished; as time passed she spent more and more of it in this pretty little room. And more and more of the time she spent there she used looking out of the window at the orchard and remembering how it was when she was a little girl.

One year, spring came again as usual, and the white frothy flowers leapt onto the branches of the orchard trees and were suddenly, surprisingly much more lovely than the perfect blossoms painted on the silk on the walls of the little room. By this spring The Beautiful Princess Kalito was spending so much time in her little room that she could not fail to notice the peasant women who came to work in the orchard. Tall young women with dirty-yellow faces, not little and beautiful at all, with eyes heavy and dark as though their craftsmen had used his thumb instead of a paintbrush. The young women came to the orchard on long strong legs with hard bare feet. Some of them carried their babies on their backs and laughed and sung to them while they cut the bright spring grass which was sprouting energetically around the trunks of the trees in the orchard. As they worked they sang — sometimes loud rough songs and sometimes sad songs, or one of them would cry or shout and the others would tease or comfort her according to rules which The Beautiful Princess Kalito could not understand. Sometimes their roughness and abuse, or the anger with which they slapped at their babies' fat legs appalled her, and sometimes their energetic cruelty made her giggle. But whether or not she could understand, whether or not she liked what she saw, she still hung against the window of the little room and watched and watched them. And when she saw their strong muddy feet with proud straight toes moving naked across the grass; when she saw one of them wrap a strong arm round another or heard them break into song again, she would feel that strange cord which she had almost forgotten tighten again, not in her stomach now but round her throat and her heart, but gradually as strong and tight as ever before. And as though the cord were pulling her together she started thinking new thoughts — about poverty and luxury and herself and the other women, thoughts that she hardly knew how to think. One day she went to her jewel chests and reaching in with her fist drew out a handful of gems. The cord was tight and almost hurting her and she scuttled and toddled as fast as she could and threw the jewels out of the window to the women below. But the singing stopped abruptly and they looked up askance, fearful, mute. The jewels were still lying there, bright and beautiful, when the women went silently home. Then The Beautiful Princess Kalito realised that it would have been better, safer, wiser, to have thrown them down food, bread and fruit, which would need no explanation, but she found she had none to throw and she did not dare to ask for any. And the cord in her throat grew tighter.

The blossoms fell from the trees and instead they were green with a sweeter more translucent green than any of the paints on the walls of the palace: a green that was never flat and smooth like the green jade bijouterie in the beautiful rooms, but soft and musical in its changes. And then from where the blossom had fallen the cherries sprang — first green too, then the colour of cream and finally turning to a richer red than the mouth of The Beautiful Princess Kalito had ever been, even in the first days of her marriage when it had been stung to fire by the passion of her husband's teeth. Then the women came back for the harvest and worked all through the day and into the night, when they would light lanterns that glowed like benign stars. Though the women shouted of their tiredness and moved sometimes with a slow weariness that hurt, they still worked on their long feet and they still sang and joked to one another. And the cord tightened and tightened again inside The Beautiful Princess Kalito until she knew that something was going to happen.

And something did. Afterwards of course they said it was the Woman Madness, the lost craziness that comes to women when their blood is no longer drawn off once a month but stays inside them to rot and fester their minds. They said that seeing herself old and wrinkled was too much for her to bear. They said that her sons' wives had not always been kind. They said there had always been bad air in that little room and that she should have been warned. They said her maids had not been loyal to their master, her husband. They said that it just went to show. One day as The Beautiful Princess Kalito watched the women and their beautiful feet busy at the cherry harvest she could stand it no longer. She left the window and tottered back to the silk cushions. She sank down on them. She looked at her tiny white feet with loathing, and tore off the white knitted over-socks. Then she ripped away at the bandages. And although the stench was as strong as ever and the room had not been filled in advance with unguents and the sweet smell of herbs, The Beautiful Princess Kalito did not even notice the evil rottenness — from the orchard came the odour of sunshine, of ripe cherries and of women's sweat. She threw the bandages behind her without even looking and as the women outside began to sing a bright brave song The Beautiful Princess Kalito, a child again, clambered to her feet to run in a renewed freedom back to her window.

When she had taken perhaps two paces the pain began. There was always some pain in walking — a dull ache which she had grown so used to over the years that she did not even know it was pain. But this was totally different: her unbound feet were exposed to a pressure which they had never experienced before; the rotted flesh, the ruined muscles, the distorted tendons could not carry even the delicate weight of the shrivelled old Beautiful Princess Kalito. After four paces she knew she would never reach the window even though the room was a small one and softly carpetted. After five paces she began to scream. She could not see the women in the orchard and she could not stop the screams.

There, halfway between the memories of sunlit orchards with the tough reality of the women who worked there and the pile of putrefied bandages The Beautiful Princess Kalito was suspended, screaming, screaming, screaming.

The screams detached themselves from her captured body and took embodiment from the air. They arrested the women in the orchard, swooping around their ears, careening out above the trees and preventing the work from continuing. The screams smashed down the corridors and spaces of the extensive palace, reverberating against the delicate jade, staining the painted walls, dumbing the musical gardens. Even when The Beautiful Princess Kalito fell to the ground in her pretty little room the screams did not cease; even when they rushed in and found her there, broken, unconscious, the screams did not finish . . . and they have not finished yet. I told you it was long, long ago and far, far away, but that might not make it any easier.

The Lady Artemis

THE NOTE OF the hounds' belling changes as they break out of the steep sided valley and set off across the open moorland. Free from the trees, the sounds unmuffled by the noisy stream, their baying seems thinner but clearer. Amid the strong vibration of hounds on a hot sweet scent is mixed the occasional yap of distress. The instinct to hunt has taken them over and yet they know that something is not quite right.

The stag's head, face on, with the high spreading antlers resembles the inside of the woman he flees. Does the stag know this? Instinct takes him too, the panic of the hunted, the power and thrust of the long hind legs, the desperate pounding beneath the rough hair on the deep chest. And yet — the eyes are not the liquid dark eyes of a deer; they are the eyes of a terrorised man who does not understand what has happened, who knows that all the world is craziness and panic and fear.

When all is silent at the bottom of the valley the Lady Artemis turns again to her bathing. Her toes are splayed wide and firm on the rock, but now she lifts one foot and steps down into the pool. It is not deep; the water comes only slightly above her knees, making a second dark triangle of water, below the smaller dark triangle of hair. The force of the water is considerable, making creamy foam garters on her lower thighs, but she does not look as though she was worried about slipping. She bends forward grace-fully, untying the ribbon from her short black hair. The snake tattooed on her spine curves with her, as though alive. Her hands reach for the water and splash it up against her breasts. The light, filtered through the green leaves of the trees and soaked into the copper coloured floor of the glade, has a curious quality of stillness, almost eerie. It is high noon and hot above the valley, but down by the stream there is no time. The waterfall behind her crashes noisily, continuously, spraying her buttocks with icy water; none-theless the effect is of complete stillness, stillness and silence.

When a small bird chirps above her in a tree there is something shocking in its noise. In the slowness of the moment of her bathing the leaves of the beech trees turn away from summer growth and incline towards the autumn, towards death and winter and retreat and rebirth. The sun continues to shine. Whether or not the Lady Artemis is aware that anything has happened is not clear.

Across the moor, miles away now, the ancient drama is played out. The hounds are good hounds; the love and enthusiasm of their owner has seen to that. They follow ever closer, the excitement of the kill urging them forward. They are baffled only because this stag does not turn at bay, but stumbling keeps on running, not towards the sea and sweet death by drowning, but towards the city.

Actaeon, rational thought destroyed by fear, and by the stag he is becoming, reduced to instincts and instincts divided against themselves, is seeking the arms of his mother. But it is too late. Alce, the lead hound, the beautiful bitch, his pride and darling, the sweet love of his life, snaps at his rear haunches. Her teeth find flesh. He does not feel so much pain as terror. The foam scudded along his flanks flies off as he turns at last. The stag turns, but the man cannot, for a brief second too long, bring himself to attack his own favourite bitch. She clings on, undaunted. The pack are upon him. He sinks to his knees, his noble head swaying despairingly. He falls. The hounds, hysterical, roll with him, tearing at his gut. Suddenly there is blood everywhere. There is no huntsman to call them off; they have never experienced the hotness of living meat. Alce, the lead bitch, so obedient, pauses, waiting for the loving sting of the thong that will call her off and will leave the stag edible and dignified in its death throes. When the instruction does not come she is frenzied. The whole pack goes berserk. The stag is dismembered, disembowelled, inaccurately, hotly, pieces are spread across the moorland. The blood is hot and sticky. There is hide, and entrails and gut and gore and gobs of foam. Beyond the pain and terror there is nothing. Somewhere in the maelstrom of blood, it all goes away. Actaeon is devoured by his bitch pack, while the dog pack in the kennels below howl dismally as they catch the savour of the killing on the hot midday air. His blood cousin Pentheus will be torn to pieces by a bitch pack too, in a similar bacchanal fury and the lead bitch will be his own mother. Actaeon is spared that at least. As if he cared.

Actaeon. That graceful boy. For after he is dead it is easier to remember him as a boy, a charming child, than to allow that he had become a man, beautiful, strange, withdrawn and arrogant. A man fully grown and fully responsible. The gossip was kind to him afterwards, as it sometimes can be when the truth is too awful. Actaeon, the prince, son of a noble line. What had he done to deserve this? It seems unfair. But the Lady Artemis does not deal in justice. It is not a cause that interests her.

But Actaeon had loved the virgin goddess. He had dedicated himself to her. He ran from the gaudy palaces and sought her places. He hunted her forests and loved her wild things. Like many true hunters he loved the animals he killed; he knew and respected them. He would rise before dawn, moving shadowy through the deserted city, and climb towards the falling stars to shoot duck as they rose from their nestings on small high lakes in the hills. He would watch entranced by the creeping of the morning. Stare as the blacker shapes of the hills sucked in the substance of the night leaving the air grey. And later, the world fully lit but colourless in complex shadings and gradations of whites, through innumerable greys to the blacks. And the colour coming in slowly, pale through creams and pinks to gold. He would crouch in the marshy places beside the lakes, delighted to shoot his arrows at the rising duck, and as delighted just to see them take sharp wing against the morning and fly away. He would walk on the beach in the afternoons, and squat for hours watching the minute, private life of a single rock pool, its busy secret comings and goings, while the waves crashed in his ears and he forgot the greater fish he had come to spear swimming brave and weightless in the deep water world off the point. He would walk the forests at night just to watch the fox-cubs, Her furred children, bundle out of their holes and frolic in the pastel light of the moon, Her moon. He had despised the bright evenings of Thebes, the noisy, laughing, chatting, singing city; he thought himself too wise, too pure, too free. He dedicated himself to the Lady Artemis.

He thought he worshipped her, and never knew until the end that he worshipped his own fear and enthroned it as a goddess and called it chastity.

And he had good cause to fear, poor child. He had seen his own mother's sister, Semele, the loveliest of them all, burst into flames and be consumed by her own passion. Burning, burning there in the courtyard of the most civilised palace in Greece, burning until there was just a small pile of dry ashes, and farewell to the lovely Semele. He had seen Dionysius, the child she bore at such cost, grow up in debauchery and glory; outshine them all, those beautiful sons of beautiful mothers, grow wild and corrupt and, damn him, joyful; nourished by the fires that had devoured his mother, destroying her to sustain himself, and rejoicing drunken, delirious, uncontrolled, dangerous and godly. Actaeon aspired to no such splendid frenzy; he sought the cool of the night and refused to hear the keening of the wind and the wildness of his own lusts. He and his cousin Pentheus clinging together, the last bastions of sanity, they were sure, of order and decorum and safety — had not their grandfather Cadmus, the founder of Thebes, brought the arts of writing to Greece and established himself and his family by wisdom and calm cunning.

But perhaps best not to think about Cadmus, the old king in his senile raving, who in his dreams and deliriums was still searching for his beautiful white sister Europa, stolen away across the sea. Searching, searching and never finding, so that there was nothing feminine, nothing sweet and light and lovely left in his life, and he could not look at his own wife without weeping. So what to remember instead, in that golden tangled court? The crazed jealousies of his uncle who had dashed his own son to death against the wall? Ino, his aunt, hurling herself and her other son into the sea and drowning to protect herself and him from her own abandoned, greedy, ambitious loveliness.

And something else. Sons do not tell how they come to pity their mothers. Sons must not say how they come to hate their fathers. Actaeon never told: following Eurydice through the green fields, playing in the grass, among the flowers. The child how small, how tender, how darkly curious, following his beloved, his adored father. Actaeon's father: a man as distant and proud and strong as his son was to become, bred in the southern deserts and always travelling on, a great hunter himself and something more, a keeper of bees, a singer of songs, a pauser, one who stops only to amuse himself. But Actaeon has always amused him before, he has liked taking his son out hunting and teaching him the ways of a man — the little boy, his mouth still damp and sweet, to be taught that women are weak and need not be accounted to, worth only a laugh. And his beautiful mother Autone, so fraily lovely and sweetly loving, and his father choosing instead to hunt the full-blown blousy Eurydice. And in the green field, among the flowers, his father's clothes abandoned beside her clothes, like brighter heavier flowers shot with gold and giddy perfume, and his father leaning over slowly, so slowly, and the child watching crouched in green grasses which tickled his nose and he must not sneeze, and the white legs reaching up to encircle his father's hips, and his father's buttocks plunging, and the two backed beast alive and writhing in the green field, among the flowers. His father's hard buttocks and Orpheus forgotten strumming his lyre at home; his father's buttocks leaping uncontrolled and his lovely mother paling, saying nothing, and a small child with a secret, for it is as evil and secret for a child to see as it is for a child to act. And now he does not remember that he remembers.

No matter. He thought he was chaste, he thought he was pure. He built a small shrine in the woods, and the Lady was worshipped there, smooth and white and cold, a little gentle smile and kind white hands, and her proud long-legged dogs at her feet. Should he have remembered other things? The screaming in the women's place, the dark opening, the space between pink and stretched wide, and the emerging head damp, dark, mysterious, and the birthing. That she, the Lady Artemis, was there and singing with the women then. She brought the women her fierce virgin self, and the power to birth their children in; she brought her space, her un-heldness, her freedom, her wild energy to their heavy work under the dark archway where a man can never stand. Should he have remembered, when he worshipped his pale silent goddess, the young girls coming back from the forest, laughing, turning away from the boys who only days before had been their playmates, and now they contained within themselves a secret knowledge and their faces were smeared with brown blood, and they were proud, and excited, and embarrassed, and wild, and secretive. They came back from their rite of the Lady Artemis changed and empowered with the strong ritual of blood letting and no man could go with them and see what they had seen. And should he have known that when her moon careened wild and untamed across the winter sky, and the young bitch wolves not yet come to their first season, would howl and growl and come down on to the sheep folds in an orgy of random bloodthirstiness and killings without sense or hunger, that this too was the work of his double-dealing white lady.

Should he have sensed that there were better and safer goddesses for fearful and frightened young men; goddesses who would be tender to such mothers' sons, but that she was huge and free and bloody and not interested at all in the plight of any young man? But he did not acknowledge his own fear; he was foolish and brave and arrogant like many fathers' sons.

He did not know, but he should have known. So he was neither innocent nor guilty when he sought her. Innocence and guilt are no concern to the Lady Artemis. Justice is not a cause that interests her.

It is hard to know what happened. It is a secret between them. She will not stay to tell and he is gone, shredded and strewn across the moor by his own bitch pack. He went out early, full of joy, five pairs of hounds lolloping happily round his heels — lean, lovely and loved, carefully bred, crossed Spartan and Cretan hounds, their mixed ancestry showing in their oddly brindled coats, the advantages of the cross not showing until they started running on a strong scent; then their tirelessness, graceful speed and full throated cry reveals the finest hunting dogs in Greece. And when he sets them to run and runs with them, graceful, strong, as tireless as they, people are delighted and say the he grows more and more like his father every day. And when he hears this a coldness comes over him, though he does not remember why, and he turns his dogs to the hillsides and runs away from everybody.

He hunted hare that morning for the simple pleasure of it. The dogs break the hare and it runs, small but fast, round and about and in and out, while he stands on the shoulder of a higher hill and watches his dogs with delight as they stream out, Alce always at the lead, and their sterns straight behind them as though blown on the wind. As the morning heightens and the heat builds up they catch the pungent scent of fox and are off. He could have called them in, kept their noses to the duller savour of hare, but he does not, he runs with them, despite the sun and away over the moorland, up and down. Sometimes they check and he can come up with them, sometimes his knowledge of the terrain and the ways of foxes spare him miles of running. Always he can hear their sweet song breaking the silence of the wild places as they run further from home and he with them rejoicing. The fox is no fool, it leads the way and the dogs follow and he follows the dogs. The fox plunges off the open ground and into a steep wooded valley and the hounds follow over the edge and into the ravine and he leaps down the side after them, laughing aloud for the great delight of it all. And when the fox goes to earth he leaves it be and calls in the hounds, and they come, their pink mouths open for his caresses. Their flanks heave happily from the long run and he thinks they will all descend to the bottom of the gorge so that he can water them.

It is magical as they go down. The trees are tall, mixed hardwoods and scrub, and under the shade of the trees it is very, very quiet. Apart from the river at the bottom whose shouting they can hear, it is almost silent. The sides of the valley are so steep that he has to slither down and the dogs pick their way with their absurd hind quarters well above their heads. At the bottom is the river. A wonderful active stream, jumping and laughing over rocks, with eddies and spurts, cutting down hard and miniature rapids and dark gold pools, falling swiftly, foamily downwards. The dogs lap greedily and he sits down to watch them. Langorously almost he stands up again and man and dogs together they make their way dreamily down the valley. Once the dogs stiffen, and seeing it, he listens; inside the noise of the stream there is another grunting sound. He casts around, and to his delight finds a boar sow laying her litter. The dogs are aquiver, but he holds them with his eyes and watches. The piglets as they are born are wet and pink, the sow is heavy and open, grunting with her work. He would like to help her through this magic moment, but she does not need him. There are five little damp piglets at her dugs and another born as he watches, neatly in its little package of mucous membrane. Her snout is busy at it, her tail bent back awkwardly. When he fears that the dogs' excitement will disturb her he gets up as quietly as possible and leaves her to her work. He is in a time of perfect happiness, and contentment. There is nothing more that he would like.

He picks his way round some boulders and finds himself on the edge of a stand of beech trees; nothing grows under them but there is a carpet of fallen leaves and masts, a rich copper coloured flooring. The light in that clear space under the trees, filtered through the pale green of the beech leaves and reflecting the copper of the ground, has a curious quality of stillness. The hounds seem strangely still and peaceful. He is at the upper end of the glade, and at his feet the stream drops abruptly down a sharp waterfall to a pool deeper and calmer than those above the fall, though still neither large nor filled with tranquil water. Beside the pool there is a pile of rocks, carried down by some earlier flooding. There is a patch of grass too, bright lurid green and scattered with white flowers. Standing alone on this patch of grass is the Lady Artemis preparing peacefully to take her bath. He knows absolutely that it is she, and he watches awe-struck. She has already laid aside her quiver and bow; he can see them tidily stacked against a tree beyond the patch of green grass. Her hair which is darker and shorter than he had imagined is tied back from her face with a simple blue ribbon. Her feet which he had dreamed of as long and slender, are smaller and sturdier than that, but even from his odd foreshortening perspective he can see that her legs, as they run up to the hem of her tunic, and beyond, are brown and fine and lovely. She is not white and cool, but creamy and warm. She is tall and her arms, naked to the shoulder, are muscled and strong. She looses the knot of her plain linen cincture which is wound three times round her waist and she unwinds it with careful precision. She folds it neatly and throws it behind her, so that it lies white on the green grass. Then she bends forward slightly, takes her tunic in both hands a few inches above the hem and pulls it up over her head. For a brief moment therefore Actaeon sees her naked body, but cannot see her face. The horror comes, the sweat wringing fear. Her body is not long and white and boylike as his imagination had drawn it; it is rounded and full-bodied. From the point of each nipple her breasts are tattooed outwards in scarlet spirals; her belly is more curved than the flat tautness of his dreams, and just below her slightly protrudant navel is a scarlet cross; the triangle of her pubic hair is dyed red and into it is carved and stained a redder lozenge. She is the grunting birthing sow, she is the wide pink mouths and stained fangs of his bitches, she is the power he feared always, dark and untamed, unpossessed, undefeated, unknown. The power that is broken and bent in the women of Thebes, here free and flowing, devouring and uncaring. Uncaring — neither good nor evil, neither secret nor open, neither gentle nor fierce. Indifferent. She does not care.

And his fear is palpable so that she knows she is observed. The hounds whine at his feet as she pulls off her tunic and looks up. The bitches, ignoring him, leap down the waterfall, all ten of them, a glorious single pounce like the water. They fawn against her body, leaning up, hiding the triangle and the lozenge, licking the belly and breasts. She looks at him, straight, and his panic rises. She looks him in the eyes. The hounds, trembling, are stilled, remaining close to her, deserting him. The beech trees do not stir, there is no wind, no noon-time, no sunlight; there is only her, looking at him. His panic surges. He cannot, he cannot bear it; the fear is sick in his mouth and shit on his legs. In its shrivelling he notices, unnoticing, that watching her unseen had given him an erection. He is animal, he is filth, he is a lie and a poison. He has seen her naked and there is no escape. He falls to his hands and knees. He pushes his head forward and moans. It is more like a roar, the roar of a rutting stag, but filled with desolation. She looks away, something else attracting her bland attention, and her hand drops down to caress Alce, his bitch, whose soft ear now lies over her wrist. She pets the hounds, not looking at him. He roars again and feels a new weight on his head. She is hunting her prey he thinks, I am her prey he thinks although she is not hunting but fondling the hounds just as he does. I am her prey. I am an animal. I am devoured. He turns to flee, to hide from the utterness of her, his legs have new strength, they are long and hairy. His head entangles in the branches. He does not rise from his hands and knees, because now his arms have hooves and they too are long and strong. The antlers are pulling his head downwards, stretching his neck. He has to get away. She will turn the dogs on him, because he has seen her naked. The hair on his face bristles, the hair on his back stands up in fear. He breaks across the glade. The stilled dogs can no longer stand it; they look to her for guidance and receive none. One of them whines. The whine restores their instinct. They turn from her, Alce leading. The first note of her hunting song breaks from her mouth as she leaps across the golden clearing. The stag is running now, beating his way up the almost vertical sides of the valley; the terror of the man at the sight of true virginity quickly replaced by the terror of the hunted animal. He knows, even as he hears the belling sound behind him that they will hunt to the death and there will be no escape. But the knowledge is wordless; he is stag now. He comes out of the valley and sniffs the upland air. He can hear the busy hounds singing joyfully at their work as they labour up the hill behind him.

He pauses, taking a great breath of air, and then he starts to run. He knows there will be no escape. He feels the bloody ending, inevitable and horrible for over an hour of hard, heart-and-lung-breaking running. For over an hour before he feels Alce's fangs sink into his hindquarters, he knows that he will feel them.

When all is silent in the bottom of the valley, the Lady Artemis continues with her bathing. Whether or not she is aware that anything has happened is uncertain. But remember it was his fear and not her malice that destroyed him, for Endymion, the shepherd prince of Latmos, saw the same thing and lay in the moonlight rejoicing and contented.

Losers Weepers

THE TELEPHONE RANG. Emma thought 'damn' with clarity, but she did not say it. Children taught one control. She ran out into the hall and answered it.

'74532.'

'pip.pip.pip.pip.pip.pip.pip.pip.pip.pip.pip.pip.pip.pip.pip.pip. pip.pip.pip.rrrrrrrrrrrrrrrrrr.'

She said 'damn'. She started back towards the kitchen. The telephone rang.

'74532.'

'Pip.pip.pip. Can I speak to Mrs Harper.'

'Speaking. O is that you Lou?'

'Yes, Mrs Harper.'

'Was it you who rang just now? These damn pay phones.'

'Yes Mrs Harper.'

'Lou, are you alright? You sound sort of funny.'

'Yeh. Yes, I'm OK. I rang to say I can't come today. I'm sorry.'

'But Lou,' Emma wailed, 'but I need you. Everything's chaotic, I really need you this time.' Then she pulled herself together. 'I'm sorry Lou, is something wrong? Is Benny sick?'

'No, thank you, he's fine.'

'What is wrong? Something's wrong, I can tell. Are you sick?'

'No. No, everything's fine, really. I'm not ill.'

'But Lou . . .'

'Look Mrs Harper, I know you need me and I'm sorry but I can't come today, maybe not this week.'

'But why, Lou?' She could hear herself sounding like a child, but Lou — cleaning the house, helping her, chatting, relaying local gossip, organising — kept her going: of course she sounded like a child, Lou functioned in her life like a mother.

'If you really want to know,' there was a note of exasperation, but perhaps also one of pleading, of longing, 'if you really want to know, he beat me up again last night.'

'O my God.'

'I look a right mess I can tell you,' she recognised the tone, a cocky bravado, part cynical, part lusty, 'my face is black and blue and I don't want to have to go out.'

'Of course not my dear,' now she was mother, Lou the little child to be treated gently, 'O Lou I do understand. Poor you, you shouldn't put up with it you know. Can't you leave or something?' The kindly but incompetent social worker voice she couldn't help recognising. If you can't think of anything practical, blame the victim, it's her own fault, she ought to leave. If one recognised these things why do them?

'It's alright. But I can't come today, I'm sorry.'

'Yes of course. But Lou . . .'

'pip.pip.pip. That's all my change Mrs Harper, now you can manage,' she was reasserting her maternal influence, 'just keep calm, don't panic. I got to go now. I'll see you. I'm . . . rrrrrrrrrr.'

O my god, she thought again, holding the telephone in her hand and looking at it. Lou was her friend, she ought to be able to do something. Battered Wives' Refuges, something like that, on the television only the other night. Probably not in the Yellow Pages. She had had qualms about a daily at first. Her mother had been in service. It didn't seem to accord with their principles. George had persuaded her. 'Emma dear, some woman needs a job. *Needs* one. We're not talking about pocket money, are we? Needs a job where she can take her children. We want to exchange some-thing we don't need — money — for something we do — a bit of cleanliness around this joint. This lady will give you something she's got — competence — for something she hasn't — cash.'

'George, that sounds like very male logic. I'd feel funny, exploitative.'

'Nonsense. Find out what the local Union rate for cleaning is. Pay that plus something and you are doing someone a favour. Right? You've got your own thing to do, and I don't want you wasting your talents cleaning my kitchen. And in any case, damn it, you're not wasting any talents at all, because look at it.'

'Clean it yourself.'

'Christ, Emma, don't be so bloody stupid.'

And so Lou had come. And somehow Lou had made it alright, with her courage and her humour and her gratitude. Lou with her face black and blue. O my God. A limited response. A real one. There had to be something she could do. Social workers, doctors, something. She could offer Lou the spare room for a week or two, so that she could have time to think things through. Not that Lou would accept. Anyway she needed the spare room. Midge and Turk were coming for the weekend. That was why she needed Lou so badly today. Get the place into some sort of order, vaguely ready. Why was she in such a state anyway? She and Midge had never minded unmade beds when they were in college, crashing out on the floor in sleeping bags if the need arose, not even noticing. What was happening to her? She watched herself attempting 'the good housewife' and was secretly relieved at her lack of success with the rôle. But still she knew she'd have to find some clean towels.

She stood, waiting, by the telephone. She felt confused. Lou beaten up. Midge needing proper sheets, preferably ironed. Herself owning proper sheets in cheerful bright prints. Fifteen years ago it would have been Lou and me, our academic differences would not have separated us yet, laughing at Midge, professor's daughter living in a posh house. Then it had been Midge and her, at college. Both a little proud of knowing each other, impressed at being able to love each other. Lou with her face black and blue. Midge married to an Important Progressive Playwright, doing historical research for the BBC. She and Lou. Midge and she. She didn't belong with either of them any more. Not now. She and George. Midge and Turk. Lou and Frank. Or another way: She and Mike and Victoria. Midge and Crispin, Alexander, Stephanie and Giles. Lou and Benny. Funny that they should breed quantatively according to class. The rich shall inherit the earth.

She went and made a cup of coffee. One thing with Lou not here she could have coffee instead of tea. She looked at the day ahead. Thought about Lou. Looking a right mess. Not that she didn't always with her hair dyed like that. Red and black and blue. Bloody cramped housing. Bloody inadequate education, so you emerged with no emotional vocabulary, no recourse but blows. Bloody lack of recourses. Was that enough? An explanation? Not really. Frank didn't fight, wasn't violent. She liked him. He was a nice bloke, he just beats up his wife when he's at home alone with her. Not alone. Poor Benny frightened out of his wits, if he had any. He was nineteen months, he couldn't walk yet and didn't crawl. 'Good thing if you ask me,' Lou would say cheerfully, 'keeps him out of mischief.' Lou thought her children spoiled, outrageous. But there was room for them to be outrageous; and someone else could contain it, cope with it. Poor old Lou. And she wouldn't leave him. With her pretty bouncy face all black and blue. I wouldn't put up with it. Bloody hell. Her face all black and blue. O my God.

She had to get on. Make a list. Clean the house. Cook the supper. Do a little shopping, no she could do that after she had picked up the kids. She had a lot of work to do too. She hated to get behind. It confirmed them in their thinking: married women are not reliable. They don't make their work a priority. We do need a commitment. 'Dear sir, I'm sorry this is overdue, but my daily's husband battered her face in so I had to do my own cleaning because we had some guests coming for the weekend and the house looks like a slum which always makes my husband look disapproving and ferocious. I am sure you will understand and I will try to ensure that it does not happen again. Yours faithfully, Emma Harper, B.A. Hons Cantab, M.Sc. (Mrs.)' She laughed, a little admiringly, at herself. In eight years she had never been late with a single job. She remembered going into labour with Vicky, and being absolutely determined that she was not going to the hospital until she had finished the job on hand. She had been furious with the child inside her for doing this to her, three weeks ahead of her careful schedule. But she had finished, even written the envelope and stuck down the stamp and made George stop the car on the way to the hospital and post it. 'You're a bloody marvel,' he'd said to her, excited by the expectation of the birth. He loved their births, holding her hand, keeping things under control; then with his arms round the baby, unwilling even to give it to her, tears in his eyes, 'you're a wonderful, wonderful woman and I love you.' Her own eyes misted, remembering.

The telephone rang.

'74532.'

'Em, darling.'

'Midge.'

'Six hundred woes. That dratted Stephanie is covered in spots.'

'O no, poor lambkin, is she alright?'

'She is, I'm not. O Em, I could wail, we were so looking forward.'

Emma realised what she meant, 'O come anyway, mine have had almost everything, spotted or striped.'

Midge laughed, 'I wish we could. But she's sickly and miserable, and I think Giles is sickening for whatever it is too. Two hundred miles in a car with two sick babies, when we don't even know what they've got. We really can't.'

'You're a traitor Midge Stewart. Here am I stuck in outer Mongolia, planning to impress my neighbours with your true London trendiness, and you don't even come.' She tried to sound light-hearted, refused to let herself plead, but she thought Midge could hear her desperation.

'Em, love, I truly am sorry.'

'O dearie, I know. It's just one of those damn things. Tell me how you are anyway.'

They started to gossip. Later Emma tried again, keeping it light she said, 'look groover, prove this famous women's liberation trip you're always on about. Leave the kids with Turk and come yourself. I want you. I need you.' Again she caught the childish note in her voice, but she felt cheated, betrayed, she only wanted to see her friends. Despite her grumbles she had really wanted Midge to come.

'Em I do wish I could.'

'Well, why not?'

'Turk's not very good with sick children.'

'O come on; I can't believe you're that bloody marvellous.' Her exasperation sounded and she knew perfectly well that George would never be left with sick children, or even with children at all, for a whole weekend.

'Look Emma, of course you're quite right, but, well, quite honestly Turk's getting a bit fed up with what he calls feminist moralising. I daren't risk it. I don't mean that, I mean he'd agree probably, he'd more or less have to, on principle. But for one horrible moment he'd look so vicious, you know. Aggressive martyr look. I hate it. For one instant I think he may be just about to hit me. O hell. That's not it. It's just as though he kept a score and whatever I do he is always winning in the virtue stakes. Damn, no that's wrong, it's more. Simply, Em it's not worth the emotional hassle.'

'Yes, I know.' And she did know utterly how nothing was really worth the hassle. 'But we must do something, get something together; I haven't seen you for months. Honestly Midge I feel so pathetically cut off.'

'Darling I do know. Here am I in the middle of swinging London and I never see anybody. When I'm not working I'm minding the kids and when I'm not minding the kids I'm entertaining boring people who my friends would hate, but are so Important to Turk's work. Look darling I must run, Turk would have a fit if he saw the phone bill: long distance, peak rate. We'll fix another weekend, you can all come down perhaps?'

They wound down with vague and hopeful plans about next time and finally parted. And the hell of it is, thought Emma, we both have bloody marvellous husbands who do what they can to help, who bath babies and sit at home so we can go out, and cook and wash up and support our desire to work. And we only have the children we wanted and planned to have and celebrated and stopped taking pills for and can afford more or less. And don't beat us black and blue. At least she hadn't started cooking yet, at least Vicky was at nursery and off her hands for a few more hours. She could catch up on her work and she wouldn't need to shop. She retreated to her desk, luxuriating in the thought of three bonus, unexpected hours that she had been given. Well they didn't belong to her, she was handing them over to her employer. But they didn't belong to the kitchen, or to George, or to the kids. At least she didn't have a personal relationship with her boss. Suddenly she knew why she had wanted Midge to come so much. It would have been her own time; Midge and she were such old friends that their husbands would have recognised this, with each other as supports they would have made a space, given the women time, they might have laughed but they would have done it, would have given them time of their own.

She justified sending her babies off to nursery school on the grounds that it gave her some time of her own, but she never made a personal claim on that time, simply handed half of it over to her husband to make his life work the way he liked it and part to her employer. She loved the kids, she loved George, she loved her analyses, but all of it was work, was duty. She wanted a holiday. But as she settled down she thought of Lou again, poor Lou. If George beat her up she'd leave. He wouldn't see her for dust. She fished out the relevant file and opened it. Her face was a right mess, black and blue. O my God.

George was casually distressed to hear that the Stewarts weren't coming. He liked them. Midge made him laugh with her sharp cruel commentary and although he had to admit he was a little bit envious of Turk's glamour and public success he really did like them both, and he knew how much Emma cared about them and it was a big drag tht they couldn't make it although actually the house would have been desperately overcrowded with four extra children around. He mixed Emma a drink, cooked supper to cheer her up and did not complain, but went quietly about the business of tidying up the mess in the house. They ate together after the children had gone to bed and he opened the bottle of wine that they would have drunk with their friends. Afterwards they sat, comfortable and giggly togther on the couch, chatting. He started to fiddle with the buttons on her shirt. To tease him she said, 'Breasts are out of bounds tonight.'

He took it as a challenge, 'They are eh? We'll see about that.' She started to do the buttons up as fast as he undid them; then when that failed she held the blouse wrapped tightly across herself. They were both laughing, looking forward to when he won: he took both her hands in one of his and held them over her head, she wriggled and kicked free, started to run upstairs, and laughing he chased her. She felt a sudden urge to win, to determine the moment of her surrender, the timing of their lovemaking for herself. But she couldn't run properly because she was giggling, because her clothes hampered her. He caught her on the landing and swung her through the air, carried her, fireman style just as he did the children, into the bedroom. She hung there, impotent and almost frightened, and when he threw her onto the bed and started tickling her, she began to feel weak. 'Stop it George, stop it now.' But she was giggling from the tickling and he didn't take her seriously, resisting was her part in the game. And it was, of course it was, she did not want him to stop, although she wanted to go on trying to make him stop. She was beginning to be turned on in any case. He had got her blouse off now and was devouring her breasts; 'I said they were out of bounds, don't you ever listen to me?'

'Yes ma'am,' he mumbled through her flesh. She bit his shoulder. But his teeth hardened round her breast and she felt herself soften. 'I want to be a tiger,' she cried but incoherently. She tried to scratch his back, and suddenly he seemed like an octopus, enormous, irresistible and everywhere: holding her chin, her arms, her breasts, pulling off her underpants. She continued to struggle, her passion mounting with her resistance. Making an enormous effort she squirmed away from him, scrambling for the far side of the bed. But he was on top of her, driving into her from behind and her mumbling protests were drowned in the pillow. And while her mind said, 'I really must object to this, he might hurt me and never know, this might as well be rape,' her buttocks lifted for him, entirely joyful, and dear God, how she wanted him, more of him and deeper.

'I want to be on top,' she said still laughing, but the laugh soaked up in her desire.

'I'm the biggest,' he said in a plausibly good imitation of their son, and he drove his twelve stone richly down into her and they laughed no more.

As he reached his climax she blurted, 'I am your tiger'. But it did not mean what she had meant before and the vague feeling almost of an anxiety she dismissed as part of her own neurosis, the result of a puritanical childhood.

Lapped in the tender delight of his afterwards, she was able to still the feelings of panic. The knowledge that she had no control over what happened once they were both turned on. She was lucky that they were both still turned on, greedily and lovingly, still, after eight years of marriage and two children. She should not ask for more. But he was the biggest. They could play and wrestle till they died but she would never win until he let her. If he wanted he could break her in half, bash her face in, and there was nothing ever that she could do to stop him. As she drifted into sleep she was struck by the thought of making love to someone smaller, lighter, weaker than herself; lifting, placing, directing, turning, handling like he did. Shocked into wakefulness she turned and tucked her head into the pit of his arm, comforted by the fact that it tightened round her, enclosed her.

She woke up with the uneasy feeling that she had been having bad dreams, although she had no idea what they had been. She lay in sleepy distress for a minute or two, when she realised that it was not her dreams that had woken her. It was the children: they were up and God knows what they were up to. She staggered out of bed, looking at George, blissfully asleep. The children never woke him; even when they were babies he had been able to sleep through their most desperate screaming. She envied him briefly before pulling on her dressing gown and hastening downstairs.

'Good morning darlings,' she exclaimed with a transparently bogus sprightliness, and suddenly they wrapped her in a love that was almost violent, kissing and hugging and leaning on her legs so that she staggered and had to collapse into the sofa.

'Steady on darlings. Who wants breakfast?'

'Me.'

'Me first.'

'No, me. I'm the biggest.'

'No one gets breakfast first sillies, you both get breakfast together.'

'I'm still the biggest.'

'I don't care.'

It was going to be a long, long Saturday.

'Look, the two of you play for ten minutes and I'll get breakfast. And don't fight.'

'Mummy,' said Mike with dignity, 'we never fight, we just play. Don't we Vicky?'

'Of course.'

At least they were in agreement with each other. She went into the kitchen, which looked faintly squalid despite formica and chrome. Mike settled down, constructing something with Lego. She loved his earnest attention. Vicky ranged round the living room for a while, and then settled down to tease Mike, probably to gain his attention. Or to play with him. Over socialised. Vicky seldom played alone. She poked him gently. He was still in a good humour and ignored her. Emma left them to it, they could sort things out for themselves, but as she put the bacon under the grill she cast an eye over them. Vicky, giggling, started to tickle Mike and he was now responding; he began to tickle her back, getting worked up. The bits of Lego flew across the room as they rolled over in a heap. Emma looked in the fridge for some milk, biting back the temptation to say, as her mother had always said — and how she had resented both the words and their truth — 'This will end in tears.' Even without saying it, as though thinking it were enough, it did. Vicky screaming, rushed across the room and into her arms.

'He's my enemy, he's my enemy. I hate him.'

'Vicky it was only a game.'

'He hurt me.'

'He didn't mean to sweetie.'

'He always wins, we always play fighting and he always wins. It's not fair.'

'But, darling, you started it, I saw.'

'I want to win sometimes. He always wins. He's my enemy.'

'Darling if you mind so much about losing you just mustn't play.'

But she knew so clearly how trite that was that she almost began to cry herself. Then the bacon started smoking.

The Burning Times

'All witchcraft comes from carnal lust which is in women insatiable.'
Kramer and Sprenger, *Malleus Malificarum*, 1486.

IN THE LONG evenings of winter the house becomes intolerable. It is too close, too smokey and too full of them, my men, my husband and my sons. Their limbs seem immense; once I looked at one of the boy's legs, spreading out it seemed suddenly half across the room, and I thought that they were once folded up and inside me, and I felt sick. When I start having thoughts like this I have to go out.

Usually I walk to the church. Tonight it is cold going through the village, with evil little winds that turn and bite at my ankles. But the cold makes precise every surface of my skin, so I can feel the edges, the limits of my body and so be alone.

Inside the church it is still. The huge rood, the suffering, broken Jesus suspended high over the chancel steps is lost in the dark, his agony mercifully not visible. There are, though, two sources of light. Far away, high on the altar the light in front of the tabernacle flickers; he is always there, watching, waiting, listening, and we cannot get away from him. Down here, much nearer, is the Virgin, the lady crowned with the sun, aglow with the light from the candles lit by women like me. I kneel beneath her feet. 'Mother, mother, Holy Mary Mother of God, help me, please, mother.' But as I say the words the tears come, and when I look up at her through the tears and through the candle flames, she seems to be on fire, the flames licking round her bare feet. She is burning, smiling, burning and I scream.

Aloud. Dear mother, let no one have heard. But she will not listen to my prayers, because I burned my own mother. I betrayed her and they burned her and I danced around her pyre. She saw me and she understood and she forgave me. So I cannot forgive myself.

And I cannot confess this sin, because they will burn me too. They will torture and break me as they did her. Then they will burn me.

The church is empty, this time. There are only her and me here. Mother and daughter. Like before.

The statue of the Virgin is in painted wood. She holds her son somewhat clumsily I feel, having held three of my own. A chance lurch of that serene head and he will fall out of her arms; she should bring him lower so that he straddles her hip, as my mother-in-law showed me, as every mother learns. I try to concentrate on that, on the dangerous way in which she is holding the Son of God; and how easy it is for a child to fall out of even the most loving arms. But the scream does not go away, and while apparently locked in prayer I am crying and remembering.

It was a long way south of here, in an altogether pleasanter valley. Afterwards I came north. My old parish priest helped me find a new place; I worked for his friend who is priest here at first. It seemed like a sensible idea. Of course no one knew what I had done, but probably they would have been pleased even if they had. But our parish priest wanted me to come away because the daughter of a witch is always in danger. In a small village they remember well. The next time it can be you.

I do not want to remember these things; nor do I want to remember the smoke filled cottage, those enormous and demanding men, and the sense of being always a stranger in a strange land. There is very little in my life that I want to remember, but though I concentrate on the precariously balanced child and the repeated chain of prayers I cannot forget that I thought she was burning, I thought I saw the flames of the bonfire and I thought that her eyes were my mother's eyes.

I used sometimes to try and justify what I did to her. What she did was an abomination to the Lord God. It was the final sin — so dreadful that it was not even named in church where every sin imaginable and unimaginable was named. So grave a sin that I did not even know it was a sin. God would have wanted her burned. But I do not justify myself any more, because even if that were true, it was not why I did it, not for the greater glory of God. No, not at all.

I blot it out you see, but it comes back. It comes back when I least expect it, when I think I am safe, like here praying in church, most piously, and I look up and I see the flames and my own mother burning.

She often seemed on fire, my mother. There was something wild in her. She laughed at everyone and at herself. Her hair was a great mass of tangled curls, and she would not smooth them down. She was a widow woman, they said, though as a child I heard other things as children will. She did not come from that village, but from another further west, towards the mountains. She never spoke of her childhood, or of what and where she had been before. She was a lace-maker; a very skilful lace-maker, and she loved the work. Our cottage was not kept very clean, she was not interested in that, my mother — not like me who wrestles with the smoke and the long muddy legs and the tight cluttered space to keep my home clean, who stays up through the night, despite my husband's calling me to bed, to shine and polish and scrub. I need the house to be clean and orderly, but not my mother, who picked up pretty things like a child and left them around to grow dusty and muddled. There was just one corner of the room that was clean and that was where her work was kept; her lace pillow with its hundreds of tiny pins bright as jewels and around them the flax threads bleached white and tied into knots that were spiders' webs and flowers and wreaths and pictures that grew magically out of nowhere; hanging down from the pillow were the bright nuts and shining stones and polished bone bob-bins. A beautiful thing, a well used lace-pillow is, and she was far the best lace-maker I have ever known. Up here they do not make much lace; one of the few things I brought with me, because I knew she would hate it to be lost, was the veil she made me for my first communion. It was the envy of the village, with the sacred host and roses and apple blossom and little violets. Perhaps it was the beginning of our troubles, for it was then that people began to say that it was not right that a poor widow woman, if she was a widow woman indeed, should flaunt her daughter in lace like a lady's in front of the whole village. The women did not like her because she did not care what they said and seldom gossiped with them. Some evenings men would come round to our cottage, wanting either to kiss her or to marry her and take her lovely lace-pillow and the money she earned home to their own houses. But she would have none of that, but would laugh at them to their faces. The men did not like her either, because she laughed at them and did not care.

To make lace you have to have very good light; so that she did not work for many hours of the day though there was spinning and washing and flax gathering of course, but as I grew older I did much of that. But when she was not working, in the early morning and the dusks, we would go out singing through the fields, and the people thought that wanton, because they had to work those fields daily. Now I know what hard work it is to be a farming family, but then of course I did not, I knew only that we went singing and laughing while others worked and grumbled.

She could tell stories, my mother. I remember that. When I tried to tell them to my sons they came out lumpish and heavy. I do not know where I went wrong, except that for her they were a joy to tell. She told them for her own joy and for mine if I wanted to share hers, whereas I told them to hush the boys when I could stand their bawling no longer; it is probably different to tell them in joyful love. Sometimes when I was small and she was telling stories, the other children would come and listen too, and on sunny evenings between hay-making and harvest even the grown-up folk would come and she would sing and tell stories. They would even forget for a while that they did not like her, because they liked her stories so well.

Perhaps I make her sound like a soft and easy woman. She was not. She was all I have said, but hard and fierce too. By the time I was about eight I was spinning for her and she would not tolerate even the tiniest flaw in the threads; she said it was an insult to her, to the work and to me myself. Spinning flax hurts your fingers, not like spinning wool which I do now easily and without thought, as I go about my work. I have never spun flax since she . . . died.

In my own head I come to it with such reluctance, so slowly. Only the thought of how close and loud it will be in the cottage, and how one of them will be wanting something of me, keeps me here at all. They cannot interrupt prayer. It is the only place for peace. But here, beneath the feet of the Mother, I cannot help remembering and all the memories pull towards the same point, the leaping of the flames and me dancing. 'Dance, for God's sake dance' said the old parish priest, who I think meant well by us always, 'dance and smile or they will burn you too.' He did not know what I had done, but I think that he held my mother in true respect; protecting me as best he could was for her. And 'dance' he urged me with his eyes and his hand, the one on the furthest side from them. I looked at my mother and all the heat and hate was gone and I knew that she knew and understood and wanted me to dance and smile and not be burned.

I was coming to woman-years. When we swam in the pools of the stream my mother would tease my new body, not harshly, with affection, but children of that age should not be teased. Even my sons I protected from their father's teasing and from each other's at that age. My mother and I were together all the time. Because the village was unsure about her, because she did not belong to them, they were unsure of me too. So I was cut off a little, slightly distant and did not have a friend. But I did not think this either a need or a loss because I had her, my mother, and she made me happy.

Then Margaret came. She trudged into the village along the road from the West, carrying a sack over her shoulder. They say she paused in the village square and sniffed the air like a dog. They say she turned three circles and marked the ground with her left foot. They say she stared at old Simon with her right eye closed. But this was afterwards when they would have said anything. And, after all, she went to the priest's house and knocked politely on the door, and he came out to her and spoke civilly with her, everyone agrees. So directed, it seems fair to assume by him and not by any other power, she walked back across the square, right through the shadow of the church tower and came down the lane to our home. It was a warm late summer afternoon, and my mother sat at the doorway to work in the soft sunshine, and her hands were like butterflies on her lace-pillow. I was beside the cottage turning the drying flax and we were singing together as we so often did. And quite suddenly my mother's singing stopped and she gave a little shriek. When I turned round there was her lace-pillow rolling in the earth, the threads unwinding, the bobbins tangling with each other and the pins bent crooked in the dirty soiled lace. My mother was running up the lane and embracing a strange woman.

They came back to the cottage together, their arms around each other, and together they went into the house. Silenced I gathered up the lace-pillow, tried to sort out the muddle and then, slowly, I followed them into the cottage. They were standing there, quite quiet, not talking, their hands on each other's shoulders and smiling. I was forgotten.

I stood in the doorway, uneasy. They turned at last, my mother with her eyes all wild and shiny and Margaret, a friend they said from my mother's homeplace and childhood. Margaret pulled back her hood and the curious reddish curls that grew quite short on her forehead sprang up uncontrolled, as they always did. She smiled at me with a sweetness like sunshine, and my confusion began.

Here in the hushed church, the cold and quiet of it, I truly cannot remember the wildness of those few months. It is this cold stillness that I want now, not that mad, fevered, triumphant, terrible time. My mother made no lace, but was up at dawn and singing, singing. She made me do my work, but never paid me any attention. Or so it seemed to me. The harvest time came and I, as every year, went out as hired help in exchange for the grain we did not grow ourselves. I hated to go out in the pale light of the morning leaving them together, but I did not know what it was I hated. I wanted my mother back, but that was not all because Margaret . . . oh Margaret, Margaret. The joy, the delight of her for me then. She had high round breasts and between them a valley deep and filled with promises I did not even guess at. She was not like my mother and I, small quick women; she was tall, big, but not heavy with it; when she walked, and especially when she used a broom I would watch the rhythm of her whole body and not know what it was that seemed so perfectly pleasing. She would sing with my mother and my own singing seemed childish squeaking. She would pick up the little pretty things that my mother would bring into the house, flowers, stones, old feathers, and just by her calm looking would transform them from pretty into beautiful. I wanted her to go away and leave us in our old closeness and comfort. I wanted her to stay, to stay near me. During the day I would follow her like a puppy-dog and she treated me like one too with casual pats and tender gestures, but laughing and happy to have me amuse her. At night the big bed seemed too small for the three of us; if my leg touched hers, or even her ruckled night shift, I would be instantly awake and aware of every inch of my skin; and yet I did not know why this was or if it was something I liked or hated. I stopped sleeping in the big bed, creeping out to lie by the hearth, but I slept no better there, straining through the night to hear her every movement, fearful and excited. She and my mother shared a secret joke that made them laugh and it drove me crazy that I did not know what it was.

So I ached and dozed and giggled and sulked and longed with longings that I had no name for. I thought they treated me like a child when I was not one. I yearned to be a child, to climb into their laps, either or both their laps, and be fondled and patted and stroked as children are. When we swam together I would watch my mother covertly, wanting her not to touch Margaret's wet, smooth body. Wanting Margaret not to follow my mother's fish-like swiftness with her eyes, wanting them both to look at me. But if they did I was ashamed of my own body which seemed ugly, gawky, childish, but which was disturbing my sleep and confusing my heart. But it was not a sad time, it was golden and laughing and joyful and I was confused.

After the harvest the lace-man came as always. He would buy my mother's lace, and look at the work of other lace-makers in the district. The prices were agreed between her and the lace-man in the presence of the parish priest, and usually my mother would come home with a glow of pride and pleasure. The lace-man would bring with him news from the world outside the village and my mother would be full of new stories and good humour. But this time my mother came back from the selling looking anxious. I thought it was because she had not done much work since Margaret came, but it was not that. She had got a good price for what she had done and had been asked for more. I pretended to sleep because I knew that my mother and Margaret would talk; I shut my eyes and lay and listened.

The Inquisitors were coming again.

They had not been to our village in my lifetime. I thought like a child that it sounded exciting, with bonfires and savage hunting, to the glory of Jesus Christ. I peeked through slitted eyes, waiting for more.

But my mother and Margaret looked like old women, hunched over the fire muttering, made small by the darkness and shadows, diminished by fear.

'We can go,' said Margaret.

'Not again,' said my mother, 'not again, I can't bear it.'

'I'll go,' said Margaret, and I wanted to cry out and stop her. 'You'll be alright if I go.'

'I don't know, I don't know.'

I shut my eyes. I did not want to see. My mother plaintive, defeated, afraid.

The days afterwards seemed darkened. Margaret did not go. She did not speak of going again, but some light had gone out of them both, and out of me. I wanted them to tell me what was happening. I wanted them to notice how their shadow had fallen on me, but they looked always at each other and with stricken eyes. I wanted to make them safe and smiling again and I could not.

The Inquisitors came. We were all summoned to Mass and a beautiful man with a white and passionate face preached to us of the dangers of hell and the perils of witchcraft, pleading with us to give up our witches, purify our community, glorify the Lord Jesus, and give the angels new tongues of praise. I remember thinking that I wished I knew a witch so that I could hand her over to him and be blessed with his smile and God's joy. And after the Mass we had a feast for our Lord Bishop's Inquisitors, who gave up their safe city lives for our protection, and who took to the dangerous highways in order to drive out the forces of Satan. It was a good feast and when Margaret and my mother went home I stayed in the square.

There was a small bonfire, and we danced around it, the young people of the village, excited by the sermon we had heard, and by the presence of strangers. At first I did not notice that something was different. Then I felt it; when I went to speak to groups of chatting people, people I had known all my life, they moved away. There was a silence where I came and it alarmed me. Then the parish priest came and took my hand and talked with me, and I thought the whole village was listening to us, and the rich clerics on their dais as well. The priest talked strangely, loudly, and with unusual affection. And suddenly I was very afraid.

When he let me go, I turned to leave the square because I wanted now to be home. The people parted for me to walk past, and when I reached the corner where our lane came out into the square I heard a disembodied voice, no one's voice, call out 'Devil's brat', and I ran.

I ran down the lane, frightened. I ran down the lane as fast as I could because I wanted my mother. I ran into the house seeking her arms. My mother was lying on our bed with Margaret and they had no clothes on and their legs, bodies, arms, faces were entangled with each other in movement, intense and intensely beautiful. When I saw Margaret's buttocks in the light from the doorway, saw them lift and plunge, saw my mother's strong small butterfly hand reach across them, spread out, holding her, then I knew what I had longed for. When I heard my mother moan softly I knew what I had wanted. I wanted to touch Margaret like that. I wanted to moan like that. I had wanted and known for months without knowing what I wanted. I crouched down clasping my own stomach in a craziness of desire. I watched them to the glorious end, Margaret triumphant kneeling over my mother, and my mother moaning and laughing, legs kicking free and abandoned, and her arms reaching up round Margaret's neck to pull her proud head down onto the breasts where I thought only I had ever lain. They had stolen this from me. Margaret had stolen my mother from me, my mother had stolen Margaret from me. Under my very eyes, laughing at me, in the face of my longing which they had laughed at. Or had not laughed at because they had not noticed in the heat of their love for each other. On hands and knees I crept away from the door out into the lane, and they wrapped in their own beauty and passion did not even hear my coming and going.

I lay for a while curled up, reaching with my own fingers as they had reached for each other, not sure what I was looking for and finding it and hating it and loving it and hating them and hating them and hating them.

Then I got up, hating myself for that lust, hating them for raising it in me, and I smoothed down my skirts and arranged my snarling hatred into a modest smile, and I walked back up the lane, burning, burning with the sight of their excitement and my exclusion from it. I walked across the square and the fiddler stopped playing and then in the silence, before all the people, I denounced my mother for a witch.

The white faced Inquisitor said I was a good girl.

When they went to hunt them up out of the cottage Margaret was gone. So they had to make do with just my mother.

They burned her.

They tortured her too and raped her and broke her. Through the next two nights we could hear her screaming. And I was afraid. I was afraid that she would denounce me, and I would burn. I was afraid that she would not and I would have to live. When they brought her out at last you could see what they had done to her. She told them that she and Margaret flew out the window at night and fucked with the Devil. She said that she and Margaret kissed the Devil's anus, and that they used his excrement to make men impotent. She said that Margaret had been made invisible by spells to escape her just punishment. She even said that the Devil made her lace for her, a web to catch Christian souls and that she transfixed the souls with her pins and weighted them down with her bobbins, the souls of babies who had just been baptised, that all her lace making was a glamour and illusion. At the end she could not stand up, but she would not denounce me though they wanted her to. She said I was innocent. And when they lit the fire and flames lept up and our parish priest told me to dance and I danced, she smiled at me. She kept smiling at me until she started screaming. Only two people were smiling though the village square was full: my mother and the chief Inquisitor, whose pale face was glowing with a radiant joy.

That time they burned three other women too, from the district. I did not know them, I did not smile. I had betrayed my mother, because my evil desires had betrayed me. But on the bed, my mother's hand on Margaret's buttock, reaching across, fingers spread out, that had not been evil. It had been beautiful.

Nothing else in my life has been beautiful. The parish priest arranged for me to come here. Afterwards I had a strange time and I could not look at fires. He was worried that they would come back for me. So I came here and I worked for his friend until my husband wanted to marry me. He is a good straightforward man, well respected. It seemed the safest thing to do, it seemed like a safe place, as far as possible from all flames. He does not worry about my occasional nightmares. He never asks any questions. So long as I do all my duties I do not think he cares.

I have three sons, but I am glad I have no daughters. I might have loved a daughter.

They say it is better to marry than to burn, but only just I think, only just.